# ORPHAN

## T.R. CONNOLLY

**Orphan**

This is a work of fiction. The names, places, characters, and incidents either are from the author's imagination or are used factitiously. The "beautiful people" of Brazil have my thanks for the joy they shared with me on my visits and for the dignity they bring to life by living it so fully.

For my beautiful bride, Kathleen

You make every day joyous

# ACKNOWLEDGEMENTS:

I don't ever recall talking about becoming a writer when I was a child, except twice:

- My uncle, Joe Lee, sat with me one afternoon at a family reunion when I was 11 and asked me what I wanted to do when I grew up. I told him I wanted to be a writer and he listened to me.

-I loved writing short stories when I was 13. Sister Julie Marie told me, "Thomas, you should write."

Kids need encouragement. It doesn't take a lot; for me just twice.

-To my reading group who made the book better by getting involved in it and making great suggestions – thanks Gerri Allegrino, Maureen Connolly, Mary Jane Cooke, Barbara Geraghty, Denise Harkins and Joe Mastranunzio

# CONTENTS

# PRELUDE

**August 20, 2016**

"Araghh," DeLuna moaned as he sat up on the floor. Soaked in blood, a chill ran through his body. He was not dead. It had been a nightmare. He had been looking down at himself in a pool of blood. Not knowing who had killed him but knowing it could have been any of scores of people. And Carlos, knowing! Carlos knew who killed him. But why didn't DeLuna know who had killed him.

The nightmare was starting to fade as all dreams do, back into the unconscious. But DeLuna would not forget this dream. It was horrible, like the one the week before when he killed the parrott, Puckerlips. He dreamt the bird had almost severed his finger and he drowned it. Well, for that, and for swearing at him all the time. Then DeLuna looked at his bandaged hand; his finger *had* been almost severed. It was not a dream—he had killed the bird. But why were his hand and chest covered in blood now? Why was there blood on the floor?

He was having trouble; his mind was under so much pressure he could not tell reality from a dream. He never had nightmares like this before. Not before the collapse of the stadium—then a series of dreams of young boys screaming for help as they hung onto the collapsing stadium, then watching them fall. Not into water but into fire. Were they falling into hell? He wondered for the first time was that him hanging on, was that him falling into the fires of hell? The dreams were getting worse, and he was having more trouble sleeping.

Was it Wednesday? He did not bound out of bed. It was a struggle; he longed for more sleep, a restful sleep. A day at the beach would be helpful. He could nap there on the sand. Only he was not sleeping, he was not dreaming. DeLuna was covered in his own blood. He had been shot. He was dying. He was losing consciousness.

The tide was going out on Chunk DeLuna. He saw himself sitting at the water's edge. He was dreaming of a day long ago.

*******

Suddenly he felt a knife at this throat. "Give me your money, or you're dead," the voice said.

DeLuna in a lightning fast move put his left hand on the wrist holding the knife, and a nanosecond later his right arm reached underneath the body of the knife wielder and flipped it over his head, smashing the would-be thief's back into the wet sand with a loud snap.

"Oowww," the knife holder hollered. DeLuna was on his chest in another second, raising his fist and then he saw the face of a teen-age boy. "Are you insane?" DeLuna said, noticing the knife had fallen from the boy's hand. He picked up the switchblade and folded it. He slapped the boy's face. "Did you hear me?"

"Ow," he howled again. "I heard you. Get the fuck off me."

DeLuna slapped the boy five more times in rapid succession, then unfolded the knife and placed it at the boy's throat, cutting it slightly and drawing blood.

A couple walking along the beach, about fifty yards away, were the only other people on the beach. They glanced at the two males and thought they might be brothers playing. They looked to be about the same size and both wore only tan khaki shorts

Gone from the boy was the bluster of a moment ago. Feeling the pain of the cut on his throat and seeing the anger in DeLuna he said, "Please, don't kill me." Fear had overtaken him.

2

"You punk, you have no idea who you are fucking with," DeLuna screamed.

The couple walking heard the rage in DeLuna's voice and picked up their pace, realizing something more than brotherly love was transpiring.

"Answer me," DeLuna said again, loudly.

"I know who you are. I see you on Wednesdays. I follow you to the hot car. I know you have money and I don't."

"But you don't know who I am?"

"No," the boy said, confused. "My name is Juan; what's your name?"

"What are you doing here? Why aren't you in school," DeLuna, the fifth grade drop-out demanded, as he got off the boy's chest.

"School? Don't make me laugh."

"What? Stand up. Let me look at you."

The boy did as he was told. He was the same height as DeLuna, muscular but skinny.

"I said what's funny about school?"

"Nothing," laughed the boy. "Except who's gonna make me go?"

"What about your parents? Where do you live?"

"Are you some kind of homo?"

DeLuna slapped the boy again, only this time not with just an open hand, further up past the palm of his hand, up the wrist. The boy went down.

"Go ahead, be a smart ass again and I'll really give it to you," DeLuna said, standing menacingly above the boy. The boy stayed down, tears formed in his eyes, but he was determined not to let DeLuna see him cry. He could not be showing weakness.

DeLuna, who thrived off of people's fears, could detect fear. He could smell it like an animal. He saw it in the boy from the tilt of his head, the position of his hands. His fingers planted in the sand would not push to let him rise, and when the boy looked up, DeLuna saw the gleam of tears being held back.

"Get up, you baby," DeLuna screamed at him.

The boy began trembling—from fear, from lack of food, from weakness.

"I'm sorry," he said as tears streamed down his cheeks.

DeLuna stood face to face with the boy who was now sobbing. The boy leaned into DeLuna, putting his head on his shoulder and began crying.

**********

DeLuna, the soul of compassion, let the boy lean on him for a moment.

"OK, stop being a baby," DeLuna said, pushing the boy back not having embraced him. "Sit down."

Once the boy sat in the sand, DeLuna sat beside him. Viewing the two figures sitting on the beach from behind, the difference in them became more apparent. DeLuna was almost twice as wide as the boy.

"So you want to be a tough guy. Where'd you get that knife?" DeLuna said holding the weapon out before him.

"I took it."

"From who," DeLuna asked.

"From a store."

"That's stealing. When you take it, that's beating someone up who has it."

"Huh?"

"There's a difference."

"I don't get it."

"You have a lot to learn."

"Can I have my knife back now?" the boy said, now standing up.

"Sit down," DeLuna commanded. "It's not your knife. It's mine. I took it."

The criminal and the would-be criminal sat in the sand talking as the tide receded another two hundred feet. In the middle of Boa Viagem beach, two hundred feet from the water and two hundred feet from the coco-frio stands along the boulevard, they talked. Just the two of them, they talked for three hours; first how the boy came to be here this day and then more broadly about life. It was a conversation in Chunk's life that had stopped twenty years before. When Chunk was fourteen, the narrative of his life changed; he became who he was today when he met Carlos, Raphael, Pedro, and Paco. His life had been unformed to that point. Then at fourteen he morphed into the gang leader, then the gangster he would become. For a moment on the beach he wondered, what if. What if he did not meet those boys that day and become their leader. Here was a boy much like himself. Which way would his life go from here?

"Your name you said is Juan," DeLuna said to the boy.

The boy sat quietly, not speaking.

"And where are you from?" DeLuna said.

"Manaus," the boy said.

"Manaus," DeLuna replied, not a question, just repeating the word.

"Yes," and Juan added, "you probably never heard of it. It's in the jungle."

"What do you take me for?" DeLuna said confidently. "Of course I've heard of it. Been there many times."

"You have?" the boy replied.

"So what are you doing here?" DeLuna answered the question with another.

"My father, he worked on a banana boat that worked the river. He took me with him, and when we got to Belem, he didn't want to go back."

Remarkable, thought DeLuna. Another father who took his son and put him in the same fix. "So, where's your father."

"He's in Belem."

DeLuna knew Belem, knew its seedy side where he owned multiple bordellos, an ocean going casino on a former cruise ship and a drug operation that covered all of far northeast Brazil. Where the Amazon opened into the giant delta between Macapa and Belem, DeLuna had a major criminal enterprise, second only to his headquarters in Recife.

"Why aren't you there with him?" DeLuna pressed.

"It's a long story." Juan said, and dropped his head.

"Don't be a smart ass," DeLuna growled. "You're too young to have a long story.

"Almost fourteen."

"Almost dead, pulling a knife on me."

The boy shrank away from DeLuna who had been sitting with arms wrapped around his knees. There was a pause—a silence that gave them both an opportunity to continue their conversation.

"Begin," DeLuna said after a time.

"He was out of his mind. He hated the jungle, hated harvesting bananas. He was right about that," Juan said. "It was backbreaking. He had me doing it with him for the last year."

A vendor came by on a beach bicycle with a large chest fitted across the handlebars. He offered sliced meats and drinks and both got a stick, a kabob-like stick of beef. Chunk got four beers and gave one to the boy.

As the vendor rode off, the boy said, "He didn't ask you for any money?"

"He knows me," DeLuna said, gnawing at the meat.

"How's that?"

"It's my beach. I let him sell his stuff here."

The boy looked at DeLuna and smiled. "This isn't your beach.

"Yes, it is."

"It's a public beach."

"Yes. I let the people use it."

"You're crazy," the boy said and Chunk backhanded him.

"Ow, that hurt," he yelled.

"Continue with your story."

Juan ripped a piece of meat from the stick, thought for a moment and began again.

"We'd climb the trees, cut the stalks of bananas, load them into carts, put them on the boats, go down river with the boat's owner, unload all of the bananas, push carts to the market, and sell them. I hated it."

"What plantation were you working for?"

"We didn't work for any one plantation. We worked for the boat owner."

"That doesn't make sense."

"There were four other guys like my father on the boat. They all had connections to banana plantation foremen or security guards. They'd let us come in, take hundreds of bunches of bananas for a price."

Chunk liked the sound of that, enterprising people like himself. "So what happened. It sounds like a good business."

"My father got drunk all the time—him, the boat owner, and the other four guys. Once they sold the bananas, they went out every night and got drunk."

"And where were you?"

"On the boat."

"Where's your mother."

"She died. I have another mother," Juan hesitated. It was the first time he had said that, and he continued, "My father's girlfriend in Manaus. We stay with her when we go back to Manaus."

"She lets you live like that?"

"She doesn't have a choice. My father just started taking me with him. It would be for a month at a time. It was exciting—the first time."

A breeze came up and cooled them against the heat of the afternoon sun. The silence lasted longer this time. DeLuna felt like he was in the middle of a movie. He tried to anticipate which way the story was going to go. He felt a light going on inside, like what must happen with Carlos and his thinking. DeLuna was always so quick to act, the story never developed. There was no thinking required in DeLuna's world, just action.

The boy was looking at DeLuna now. Sensing this, Chunk looked at him. He was crying, tears streaming down his cheeks.

"What happened?"

"The men on the boat with my father, they would all come back to the boat drunk, singing, yelling. Usually they had women with them. They would stay up all night screwing in the galley of the boat, right where we ate," he paused; a shudder ran through his body. "I couldn't sleep most of those nights and just stayed quiet in the room I shared with my father."

The boy began to tremble, his shoulders rising and falling.

"Did you watch what they were doing," DeLuna asked, wondering if Juan was getting an education in the sexual ways of men and women.

"No, I hated the noise. I put things over my head. Those women were screaming," and he paused. He took a deep breath and heaved. "That wasn't the worst part when they came back to the boat with women." Juan paused again, followed by sobbing and more shudders and heaving. DeLuna felt bad for the boy. "The worst part was when they came back to the boat without women."

"What was wrong with that?"

"That was when they came for me."

DeLuna's head snapped to the right. He was staring at the boy; his eyes were wide open and piercing. "What do you mean they came for you?"

"Two of the men would come into my room, the same two each time. They'd cover my mouth and have me." Juan saw the question on DeLuna's face. "You know, down there," he said pointing to his private parts.

DeLuna's head dropped in recognition and then popped back up. "Where was your father?"

"On those nights he slept in a different cabin."

"He knew?" an enraged DeLuna demanded.

Juan nodded, "He sold me to them."

The silence that interrupted their conversation would have been deafening were it not for the continued sobbing of Juan and a deep, long rolling growl from somewhere inside DeLuna.

"One night they were so drunk they were arguing outside my door about my price. My father had raised the price for me, and they didn't like it. They argued back and forth. Then it got very loud. Fighting. They killed my father and came for me. They were so drunk they didn't even close the door. As they were working on me in the dark, I could see my father lying in his blood outside the door."

Chunk moved over next to the boy and put his arm around his shoulders. The boy pulled away. DeLuna understood.

8

He told DeLuna he never saw his father again. They were on him over and over all night long. They brought the other three men in, all of them stepping over his father like he was not there. When it ended they locked him in his room. He passed out from exhaustion and woke up some time the next afternoon.

"There was no noise on the boat. I was really hurt. I figured they'd kill me that night. I had bite marks all over me, my ass was bleeding and I could still taste them in my mouth. I knew I was dead if I didn't get out."

"Jesus," DeLuna said aloud, wincing several times as the boy described his rape. "How did you get away?"

"That night they got lucky. They came back with women. After the women left, I heard the door open. I reached for my knife.

"This knife," DeLuna said, holding it up.

"Yes. As the door opened, it was dark, but I could see that it was only one of them. He was being very quiet. He stepped in and closed the door. It was totally black in the room. He stumbled across and fell into my bed on top of me. I started telling him no and he said "quiet."

I stabbed him in the back. He started to make noise, and I cut his throat. The sound stopped, but he was a gusher. Bled all over me. I fished in his pockets and found money. I crept out of the room and up the stairs. No one was awake. I got off the boat, went down to the beach and stayed in the ocean trying to wash them and the blood off me."

"Grim, very grim," DeLuna said, his jaw tight in disgust. Juan continued sobbing.

The sun was lower in the western sky as DeLuna and the boy faced east to the Atlantic. They sat in silence as the wind picked up and a chill shook Juan.

"When I asked you before where your father was, you said he was in Belem. Why didn't you tell me he was dead?"

"He is in Belem. If I told you he's dead, you'd ask a lot of questions," Juan replied, leaning forward, wrapping his arms around his knees and placing his chin on his arms.

"I asked a lot of questions anyway," DeLuna said, wanting to move forward. "When was all of this?"

"About three months ago."

"Did you go to the police?"

"No."

"Why not? They killed your father."

"Why? They were probably gone once they woke up and saw I got free. I'd probably be in jail for killing one of them."

"No, no, you were innocent," DeLuna protested, ready to defend the boy. "You only did what you had to do to survive," Chunk empathized.

A brief silence occurred and DeLuna asked, "How did you end up here. Belem is a long way away."

"Truckers. Different truckers," Juan said staring out to sea, then turning toward DeLuna, "I wasn't looking to come here. I just wanted to get away from there. After a couple of days in different trucks, I had no idea where I was headed. But I did keep seeing signs on the road, "Recife." So I kept heading this way. I heard about Recife. I knew it was a big, rich city. I've been here six weeks now."

"And you are still all alone, no gang?"

"Not yet."

"How do you live?"

"Begging, robbing. I've had you pegged from the beginning. Every Wednesday you come here. Then I followed you a couple of times to your car. I knew you had money."

"Stupid. You're an idiot. You try robbing me and all I have on is shorts. Where do you think my money is? In my ears," he said handing the boy the last of the four beers.

"I was planning to follow you back to your car. But I have not eaten in three days. I was so hungry I needed the money right then."

The vendor on his bicycle came by again. Chunk asked the boy if he wanted anything.

"Sure more of that meat and another beer."

"No more beer for you, a soda, and another meat stick. Make it two meat sticks, a soda and four more beers," DeLuna said to the vendor.

Once he handed them over, the vendor in his late twenties thanked DeLuna and rode off, again without payment.

"That doesn't seem right, not paying him," Juan said.

"You want to pay him? I'll call him back," DeLuna challenged.

"That guy needs to make money. You're an asshole for not paying him."

"Watch your mouth," DeLuna growled, slapping the boy in the head and ripping off another bite. "I was just getting to like you."

"I knew it; you are a homo."

And Chunk hit him again, lighter this time. DeLuna put his food down and leaped onto the boy, started wrestling with him and began laughing. DeLuna had the boy pinned and looked down at him, laughing again. He saw someone he knew there.

The boy laughed too. He could not recall the last time he laughed.

**********

Thirty-six years before, Raul DeLuna left his native Recife to work for a rich engineer who wanted a houseman for his family as he moved to Puerto Rico to build condominiums along Isla Verde Beach. Raul married a Puerto Rican girl and had two children: a girl, Silvana, and a boy, Juan. His wife died in childbirth with Juan. He raised the children with Silvana's Puerto Rican Aunt Carmen.

Raul DeLuna was not committed to Puerto Rico, and when the opportunity came, he took his son and returned to Brazil, leaving his daughter to be raised by her maternal aunt. The circumstance of DeLuna's leaving occurred during a sleepover with his daughter, Silvana, and her girlfriend, Santa Alba. Fourteen-year-old Santa woke in the middle of the night to find DeLuna's thirteen-year-old son, Juan, on top of her, prying her legs apart. She screamed. The incident would have been just that, but then Santa Alba, the young beauty queen of Coamo, began talking about it, enlarging it. Juan "Chunk" DeLuna became a pariah in the small mountain town of Coamo. It is astonishing how fast word of mouth spread, even before the age of social media, across a town of twenty thousand people; how a curious sexual search by a thirteen-year-old boy became known to more than half the population; and how that searcher was labeled "child molester" even though he was a child himself.

After several months, unable to change the narrative, rehabilitate his son's reputation or calm the anger in his own daughter, Silvana, he took Chunk and left. He was unable to make peace with his children's Aunt Carmen, who held Raul accountable for his son's behavior. "Ever since his mother died, you have a different slut in your bed every night. What's the boy to think?"

It was not a good time to return to Brazil. The country was mired in recession; jobs were scarce. Raul took the only job he could find—on a banana boat working the Amazon plantations. He set up a home base in Manaus with a girlfriend, and when his girlfriend tired of taking care of his son, Chunk, as Raul was gone for weeks at a time on the boat, he brought the boy along with him. Juan was thirteen years old; he could help with the work on the boat. And that spelled doom for Raul: he was murdered by his co-workers on the boat, haggling over the price Raul would get for selling Juan as a sex slave to those men. Escaping from his "prison" on the boat, Chunk DeLuna began fending for himself, initially asking and begging, then stealing, and finally starting his gang. Chunk DeLuna would not go hungry again.

# PART

1

## April 15, 1996

Recife, Brazil, is that point in South America that juts furthest east into the Atlantic Ocean. If Pangaea, the original supercontinent of earth, were put back together, Recife would tuck nicely into the African country of Cameron.

The sky above the city of Recife is filled with clouds. The clouds come in columns, like they were puffed out of a great chimney. Straight as arrow columns, then rows of them. But not too far inland, mainly along the coast, they float along like a quiet army.

The boy sits on the sand of Boa Viagem beach looking at the clouds, thinking about them. He is the only figure on the beach on this cloudy day. The boy is sitting there in tan shorts with no other clothes. It is not that he is going swimming; these shorts are all the clothes he has. He sits with his arms wrapped around his knees.

A dog has been swimming and now, emerging from the surf, notices the boy. He shakes the water off of his long, short body. It is like a chain reaction; the water flies off in small beads, beginning at his head and progressing all the way down his body.

Chunk smiles as he sees the dog looking at him. The dog notices the smile and comes slowly to the boy and sits beside him. The two sit on the beach, not communicating, just each with their own thoughts, beside each other.

After some time, the dog gets up and walks off. He stops once and looks back at the boy. Then the dog turns and goes further down the beach before heading to one of the seaside carne-de-sol stands that specializes in sun-dried beef. Usually the dog can count on the owner for a scrap.

The following day the boy Chunk is walking across the Sao Antonio Bridge, which crosses over the Juquia River as it flows to the sea. The river is a filthy brown cesspool carrying all the elements of city trash: papers, boxes, plastics, rubber, fruit, vegetables, and occasionally dead birds. Pieces of clothing float lazily on top next to tree branches.

At this moment late in the afternoon, four brown mulatto boys, clad only in the same type shorts as the boy, are running on the far side of the bridge, their shoe-leather-like feet scurrying across the hot cement. They have hold of the same dog that sat beside Chunk the day before. They lift the dog up and toss him in the river. Then the four boys climb the cement rail and one by one dive into the ooze after the dog. All five swim to shore and climb back up to the street to once again escape the steaming humidity by launching themselves into the river.

As the boys grab for the dog, he barks, then snaps at them, trying to escape their grasp, but longing to be with them. As the four mulattos get their hands on him by grasping one leg each, Chunk approaches them. He is smaller than the other four but about their age, somewhere in the early teens.

"Ola," he calls. "Put the dog down."

The tallest of the four boys looks over his shoulder and laughs, "OK, boys, let's put him down—in the water." They proceed to launch the mangy cur into the slime.

The new arrival runs to the rail and watches as the dog struggles to get to shore.

The older boy approaches Chunk and tells the others, "Now let's throw this nosy dog in."

As they all laugh and start to move in on Chunk, he promptly flattens the older boy with a punch squarely on the nose. With lightning speed and a face now twisted into a battle glaze, looking more bull dog than human, he rapidly punches and kicks one, then another, until all four boys are down on the cement bridge at once.

He does not say a word; he turns his head and walks away. The four boys, not sure what hit them, all get up and watch as Chunk heads in the direction of the beach. The dog now back up on the bridge, looks at the four boys, and then looks at Chunk. After weighing his options, he follows Chunk.

Chunk walks to and then along the beach that has many bathers in the water this day. He finds a place to sit. Walking along the beach about fifty yards behind him is the dog and about another fifty yards behind the dog are the four boys.

Chunk DeLuna is fourteen the day he meets his new friends. He has been in Brazil for nine months. His father, who took him with him from Puerto Rico, died violently six months after they came to Brazil. And for the past three months, Chuck has been living along the beach, sleeping on the beach, or when rousted by the police moving under the piers in the harbor. But now he is no longer alone. He has a dog; he has a group of four new friends who have come to sit beside him.

"Where did you learn to fight like that?" asks Carlos, the older boy, the first to be punched and the first to go down.

"My father taught me," Chunk tells him.

The littlest one, a boy named Raphael, with a dirty patch over his right eye says, "I never saw that punch coming."

"That's because you're blind," Pedro says, as he and his twin brother, Paco, begin cackling.

"Don't make fun of him," Chunk commands. "What happened to your eye?"

"I don't know; it got infected or something. I can't see out of it any more. When I put this patch over it, it doesn't hurt as much," Raphael says.

"Can I see it?" Chunk asks.

"Sure," and he lifts the patch up. Chunk winces. It is a mess of infection and oozing puss—red and blue and purplish.

"You need to get to a hospital."

"I've been. They clean it up for me, give me some medicine to wipe on it," Raphael replies.

"They've got to do more than that," Chunk says firmly. "I'll go there tomorrow with you." Chunk suddenly feels better than he has since his father died.

The older boy, Carlos, asks Chunk," You talk a little different from us. Where are you from?"

"Puerto Rico," he says.

"Where's that?" one of the twins asks.

"It's an island in the Caribbean Sea," Chunk replies.

After a brief geography lesson, Carlos asks him his name.

"Chunk."

"Chunk? That's different. What's it mean."

"Nothing, it doesn't mean anything," Chunk says, realizing he has no idea why his name is Chunk. He knows his given name is Juan DeLuna, but he never thought to ask where Chunk had come from.

The boys tell Chunk their names. They too are homeless, living in the basements of the public housing buildings inland from the beach.

"I used to live down here at the beach, but the police kept hassling me," Carlos tells Chunk.

"Yeah, they do that to me to, but I just move along down by the piers. Mostly it's okay sleeping along here," Chunk replies, adding, "Tonight you boys stay in my house."

The boys smile, knowing they have a new leader. Carlos has been deposed with one punch, but he does not seem to mind.

They talk the rest of the afternoon, and as the sun goes down, they move towards the street to hustle some food from the beachside vendors. The dog tags along.

"Whose dog is this?" Chunk asks.

"No one's, he just comes around," the twin named Pedro says.

"Well, he's part of our gang now," Chunk laughs and reaches back to pat the dog who growls as Chunk approaches too fast. He calms down once he realizes the boy means no harm. Chunk looks at the hair falling out of the dog and notices the mange infestation on his skin.

When they pass by a stand cooking churrasco, Chunk sees a large drum of kerosene off to the side of the stand. He quickly grabs the dog by the scruff of his neck, lifts him up and dunks him just short of his mouth in the drum. The dog howls, a screeching agony, as the open sores are filled with the oil.

"What in hell are you doing," the man cooking in the stand says as he opens a side door and witnesses the dousing.

"Dog's got the mange," Chunk says.

"Yeah, that will kill the fleas alright and the dog too. What are you kids thinking of. Get the hell out of here," he says dismissively, but not angrily.

Chunk puts the dog down, and he runs off barking at anyone who comes near him. When the boys last see him, he is running towards the water.

"Well, there goes one member of our gang," the twin Paco says.

"Nah," says Chunk, "he'll be back, and he'll thank us for it."

"You're crazy," Carlos tells Chunk admirably.

"Crazy like a garota," Chunk replies.

"Like a girl?" Pedro smiles.

"Yes, they're very clever," Chunk replies.

The sun fades, and the night approaches. The five boys walk along the beach and talk of dreams for their gang. As a couple passes by them, suddenly Carlos and Raphael hit the man to the ground and begin to pummel him.

"Give me your money," Carlos screams at him as the man's girlfriend looks on horrified.

When the man reaches in his pocket from the prone position, Chunk grabs Carlos' arm and pushes him aside. "No, this is not the way."

Chunk leans down to help the man up, "I am sorry. My friend has lost his mind. Please forgive us." He brushes the sand off the back of the man's pants and gently urges him on his way. The terrified couple's pace picks up as they head up off the beach.

Chunk slaps Carlos hard on the head, and Carlos put up his hands as if to box. Chunk promptly punches him hard in the stomach with his right hand and as he bends forward, hits him in the head with his left hand. Carlos falls to the sand; with a hand outstretched, he pleads with his attacker, "Please, boss, do not hit me again."

Chunk bends down to help Carlos up. The other three gang members hold their ground, not sure what is going on.

"Carlos, my friend, if I am to be your leader, you cannot go attacking people when I am not aware. We do things by planning them. We do not act like retarded people, just jumping on anyone passing by."

"I'm sorry, Chunk," Carlos says remorsefully.

Still later in the evening they discuss holding up a beach concession stand that will be far more profitable. Once the plan is worked out, they decide to try it out on a coco-frio stand. The person working the stand would be up front with the machete and coconuts. The twins Paco and Pedro would approach the stand from the front, appearing to buy a coconut filled with its cold milk. Raphael would keep an eye out, "one eye," Pedro says, and he and Paco are laughing again. Chunk slaps Pedro on the head and says, "I told you about that."

Carlos and Chunk, the two strongest, would come up from behind the stand and grab the vendor forcing him to the ground. Then they would take money from his pants and from under the counter. They would also take the machete the vendor used to lop off the heads of the coconuts and all five would flee into the darkness of the beach. The machete would be the beginning of their arsenal, Chunk told them. "Anytime we see weapons, we take them. We will need them in the future."

The plan works perfectly, and as they are all running for the beach, with Chunk bringing up the rear, an arm goes around Chunk's neck. It is a police officer who has witnessed the end of the robbery and waited beside a small outbuilding to grab at least one of the robbers. He has Chunk in a choke hold as he calls for help from a partner across the beach boulevard. Just as the other partner is crossing the street and the officer with the choke hold on Chunk is pulling him out towards the street, the officer screams in pain and reaches for his leg. In that second, Chunk breaks free and heads toward the dark of the beach, noticing that a small dog has clamped his teeth onto the officer's calf.

"My little dog," Chunk calls out. And with the officer now on the ground, the dog releases him and runs off after Chunk.

The five boys and the dog run into the black night toward the piers. There will be no catching them now.

Under the pier, they are all patting the hero of the night—the long short dog with the mange, or less of it now.

"We must have a name for a dog like you," Carlos says

"He looks like a hot dog; let's call him hot dog," Raphael says.

"We'll call him Shorty, Cortito," Chunk says naming his dog. "Come here, Cortito," he says now looking at the animal, who moved next to him.

"And we'll call our gang, Rei de Praia. We are the kings of this beach," Chunk raises his hands up and begins a small dance, and the other boys follow, dancing merrily not in their poverty but in their newfound wealth: the fraternity of the gang. And Cortito, wags his tail and barks with his gang.

The following day the five boys, dressed only in their shorts, and one short dog enter the Sao Francisco hospital. They go to the emergencia entrance and are told to wait along with the huddled mass of poor seeking help.

After two hours pass and no one calls Raphael's name, Chunk rises to get some attention. "No, Chunk, we must wait our turn," Raphael tells him.

"You sit down, Raphael; I'll be right back," Chunk says as he walks through the doors where other patients have advanced for treatment.

Several minutes later Chunk emerges with a doctor standing beside him. He waves Raphael forward and then puts his hand up indicating that the others should wait there.

Chunk accompanies Raphael and the doctor to the triage area, and the doctor pulls the curtain behind them. He examines Raphael, calls for a nurse and tells her several things. She brings a few instruments and places them on a metal table beside the doctor. The doctor takes a magnifying glass and a long, thin metal instrument and has Raphael lay back. The doctor turns on a bright overhead light and proceeds to look in Raphael's injured eye.

After a couple of minutes of probing, he steps back and turns the light off and says to Chunk, "Raphael has a very serious infection under his eye. We need to do a small procedure, get what is in there out, put some antibiotics in, and clean it up. We can do this later this afternoon."

"Good, we'll wait outside." Chunk says.

"No, I need you to leave. Your friend needs to spend the night in the hospital to make sure the infection is reducing. You can come back tomorrow," the doctor concludes.

"I will come back for him tomorrow at noon time," Chunk says. He walks over to the table, puts his arm around Raphael who is now sitting up, and says, "You'll be fine. This is a good doctor, and he will make your eye better. Do everything he says and do not be afraid."

"Yes, Chunk. Thank you," a grateful Raphael says.

The doctor says, "Raphael, you stay here, and I'll get you ready in a little while." And the doctor leaves.

As the boys rise to leave, Raphael asks, "What did you say to the doctor, Chunk? They have never taken this much time to find out what was wrong with my eye before."

Chunk reaches into the canvas bag he is carrying and shows Raphael the machete they had stolen from the coco-frio stand the night before. "I told him you were very sick, that you had come here many times and no one had resolved your injury. I said I was here to make sure that this was fixed today. I reached into this bag and put my hand on the machete. As I was about to take it out the doctor said, "You are right to be concerned about your friend. I will see him and look after him."

# 2

When he was nineteen, the girl he had been living with in the projects gave birth to twins, their third and fourth children. Having the babies helped DeLuna get a four-room apartment in public housing. He liked having a permanent place. He liked having sex whenever he wanted.

Suzanne also liked having a place of her own. When she wasn't sleeping with the boys under the piers, she was with her family of nine in a four-room apartment, two buildings away from the apartment she eventually got with DeLuna. Although DeLuna could be a brutal lover, Suzanne felt living with him, caring for his children, would provide her with security and freedom. After all, she felt, what else could a twenty-one-year-old with four children do?

Business for DeLuna was growing. His beach kings gang now numbered twenty-three. From robberies along the beach, the gang had graduated next to prostitution. It was easy. The gang would offer the girls who came to them under the piers to older men seeking sex. Under cover of darkness, the beach became their brothel. One hundred yards from the edge of high tide to the sea wall gave the gang room to conduct business. The only lights along the beach at night were street lamps, dim from age, yielding light no more than twenty yards down onto the sand from the sea wall. The sea wall itself was useful—every hundred feet or so along the beach the gang painted a number—for over a mile. The numbers were the

23

"brothel rooms." A man comes looking for a girl, he pays Raphael, and he gives the john a number. The john walks along the beach till he finds his number on the wall. At that point, there is a girl waiting for him, and the two walk towards the sea under cover of the black night. There is enough space where couples cannot see each other, but on calm nights when the waves are not crashing, they can hear others in passion on the dark beach.

**********

The towels were spread on the beach. They were there early as the hot sun dried and packed hard the apron of sand that stretched for seven miles. The four children were busy at play; the two oldest, two girls about five and four, were in the ocean; the two youngest, twin boys aged two, were digging in the sand. The vigilant mother, covered in a smock, sat watching all of them as a salt air breeze came in off the ocean. It was 9 a.m. at Boa Viagem beach in Recife.

The father showed up fully dressed, took a backpack off and sat on a towel. He was short, stocky and appeared edgy, fidgeting with his hands. After a few words, the mother started back toward the street that paralleled the beach. The father followed. Seeing this, the mother stopped, and one of twins ran crying after the father who did not stop. The mother, angry, picked up the two-year-old and walked to the water's edge.

She thought to herself, I've been put in my place. She walked back to the towels, kicked the father's backpack and thought again, you've got to stick it out for the kids. Your life is over; theirs is just beginning. The boy wriggled free from his mother's grasp and scampered off. The oldest girl came and nuzzled against her mother. The mother hugged her daughter—frustrated, comforted.

The father reappeared on the beach and walked by his family without acknowledging any of them. He stopped fifty yards beyond them and sat in the sand.

The mother rose, picked up the two-year-old and walked towards the man. A defense mechanism she had learned. He never hit her when she was carrying one of the children. The other

24

children all marched to where the mother now stood beside their father. He walked away, back toward their towels.

The family followed. Three of the children went off to play as the mother and father sat two feet apart with the mother continuing to clutch one of the twins. The mother, a brunette mulatto, looked young but tired. She said something to the children's father. He turned towards her and put his face within inches of hers and spoke. They exchanged words; she through clenched teeth and a tightened jaw. It was a quiet argument, dampened by the noise of the nearby surf. The silence of the argument grew on the faces of the parents. Abruptly, the father pulled the boy from his mother's arms and scooped up the other twin. With one boy under each arm, he walked off the beach to Boa Viagem Avenue.

The mother, her back to him, put her left hand to her head and began to weep. The five-year-old girl ran up to her mother, took a towel, shook it out, and wrapped her wet body in it. She looked in the direction of her father and said, "Where's daddy going?"

The mother said something. The girl wrapped the towel tighter around herself and sat beside her mother. After several minutes the younger girl joined the older girl and their mother. The two girls then began playing in the sand.

The mother stood, folded the towels up, and assembled the backpack, toys, and towels in one place. She then went and sat in the sand with her two daughters. They talked. The three of them built small sculptures of sand with plastic green and yellow buckets and shovels.

The argument had begun the night before as all their arguments had. They began at night and carried forward into the next day until she yielded. And she always did. She needed to. She needed him. He was not reliable, but somehow they survived financially.

Slowly she put sand in a bucket; the girls did the same thing with the other two buckets. Maybe, she thought, he was always on edge, snapping, because his responsibilities weighed on him: four kids all under six, a wife, an apartment, debts and an old struggling Toyota. He never wanted to come to the beach with his family. He said he liked going by himself.

As the sand structures the mother and daughters were building grew, all three recognized they had built a small city. The girls began stretching the boundaries. The mother began recalling further back in time. He was always tense. It was not the responsibility. It was just him—easily provoked, a button waiting to be pushed.

Suzanne's girl-friends questioned what she saw in him. Her mother flat-out did not like him. "He is way too different than you, honey," was the way she put it. Chunk DeLuna was different, way different. Suzanne was docile, calm, and happy. She focused on her children. He did not do much as far as Suzanne could tell—spent most of his time with his gang, his all-important gang. She was young when they met; he was younger. He did have a certain charm. Their other friends were attracted to him, but only the boys. The girls were repulsed. Suzanne did think about this from time to time and concluded it was some form of animal magnetism, animal leadership, where the king-of-the-jungle prevails and rules. They had met at the beach. She was one of the girls who hung out under the piers and like so many other poor girls went into prostitution to get money. She was one of the "wall-bangers" as Chunk and Carlos referred to the girls that Raphael ran out of the beach brothel. Only one night when Chunk was young, just getting started, she had sex with him. At the time, he was not too experienced, but she taught him, helped him. A relationship built, a loyalty, and then a family. She was one of the few girls who thought Chunk could become someone; other girls she knew were afraid of him, if not from his looks then by his behavior—thuggish, brutal, cruel.

Suzanne, two years older than DeLuna, was as stable an influence in his life as he had known, well, since his sister Silvana, back in Puerto Rico, had helped raise him when his mother died.

Things began changing fairly early in their relationship, though, as Suzanne intentionally became pregnant and had their first child when she was sixteen; Chunk DeLuna, the father, was fourteen. The trap was sprung. She would not have an abortion despite his asking her to. In each of her later pregnancies, DeLuna also asked Suzanne to have abortions. She refused, and the wedge between them grew. But he stayed with her and their children despite the notorious rate of abandonment by members of his gang for the girls they got pregnant.

How did a man, rather a boy, get like Chunk, she thought. She knew; she reasoned he had his tics and with each year that passed they became more exaggerated. What she did not see coming was the extent that he became meaner to her and more demanding to everyone, particularly his gang. As a teenaged mother, she worried about food, shelter, and clothing; her babies; and occasionally, the wild man who came tearing into their apartment each night. But now she could see that the tics were getting worse and bigger. What about me, she thought, moving the sand through her fingers, clutching at her girls. "Who am I from what I was. What have I become, staying with him, raising my children in his house?" The happy girl could still have her moments with her children. She did everything to make sure they were happy. When her mother was alive, she reinforced Suzanne by letting her know that the children were all her—lighter, happier with none of his darkness. Now with her mother gone, she was alone. She would hold together for them, but it was hard. So hard to do all she must: keeping their home, feeding the children on what little Chunk gave her to shop, cleaning, dressing, and mending. There had to be a better way, she thought.

When they first met, Chunk was exciting, even then dangerous, but exciting at fourteen years old. He had been arrested several times as had every member of his gang. Then he got a police lieutenant's amorous daughter pregnant. DeLuna was charged with statutory rape; the girl was thirteen. He was sentenced to a year in jail. Suzanne had it confirmed that she was also pregnant with their first daughter shortly after Chunk was jailed. The prison he was sent to was a dilapidated housing project that had undergone renovation of a sort: bars had been installed on windows, iron gates replaced apartment doors, and a 10-foot-high barbed wire fence was installed around the perimeter. The prison was considered minimum security. Most prisoners were incarcerated for less than two years and for non-fatal crimes.

Suzanne began visiting Chunk once weekly on Saturdays. She felt she could help him become a man; she loved him and wanted a father for the child she would have. On the long bus ride to see him, she heard her mother's words: "DeLuna is no good for you." Part of the voice inside her said run, run as fast as you can. The other part said, make him a real man.

**********

On her first visit to see DeLuna behind bars, she hoped he would see his errors and commit to reform. The first bus ride across dusty city streets, through gray, filthy second city favelas, over rural hills and close to the encroaching enormity of the deep green jungle to the west took fully two hours. It gave young street-smart, but somewhat enchanted, Suzanne time to think. "By loving a man too much does a woman become a slave to the thought of love? Can all women be condemned for the sin of Eve?" These were the musings of a sixteen-year-old girl—pregnant, poor, and thinking of a future that would take her from the present.

"What crime," DeLuna asked Suzanne.

"Chunk, you raped her; she was only thirteen."

"Did I rape you?"

"No."

"No is right. It was the same thing. She came sniffing around, flirting. She got it."

"Chunk, she was thirteen. Her parents had to have her get an abortion."

"Good for them. A kid thirteen don't need a baby."

"How about a kid that's sixteen?" Suzanne asked.

"Same thing. Who's the sixteen-year-old?" he asked, not totally engaged.

"Me."

"You! You?" DeLuna said, and anger began to rise. "Who got you pregnant?" DeLuna said from across the metal table in the large, open visiting room. He had an indignant scowl on his face.

"Yes, me," she said and then added, "Who, who got me pregnant? Who do you think?"

"No way."

"Yes, you. I have not been with anyone else since our first time." Suzanne said somewhat proudly. "Chuck, this is a good sign. We can begin our family."

"Are you nuts. You do what that other bitch did. Get an abortion. I don't want any kids."

"Chunk, I love you. I am going to have our baby. This is a good thing, you being here. It can help you turn around so you don't get in trouble again."

"Suzanne, we get along good; don't screw it up. I'm not having a family, a wife, or a kid and being here will help me. I'll be smarter in the future, smarter about everything. Once I am out of here, I will never spend another day in jail."

"I am glad to hear that. And I think I can change your mind about us."

"You can try. You're a beautiful girl, Suzanne, and you screw great, but get the idea of the baby out of your head."

"No. I'm having the baby."

DeLuna growled; he stood up. "Kill the fucking kid or I will."

The guard at the end of the room shouted, "DeLuna, sit and be quiet."

Suzanne was not shocked by DeLuna's outburst. He was that way, but she was hurt. "I'm leaving now, Chunk. Don't talk to me like that anymore or I won't come."

"Oh, did I hurt your feelings?" DeLuna laughed. "Too fucking bad." He raised his hand and pointed a finger at her, "You kill that kid."

"No," she said and she rose and left.

Suzanne did go back to see DeLuna, several times, but each time he was just as abusive. Towards the end of his one-year confinement, he seemed to relent when she was no longer pregnant. She was a mother; he was the child's father. During that time, she got by with help from her father and public welfare, which got her a small one-bedroom apartment since she had a baby. The baby girl was born four months before DeLuna was released. Suzanne was sixteen; Chunk was fourteen.

*********

DeLuna came back to the beach, packed his wife and four children into the old Toyota and drove them home, some two miles away from the beach. On the way, he called Paco on his cell phone. "Meet me at my house at seven."

"Why is Paco coming to our house tonight?" Suzanne asked.

That night twenty-one-year-old Chunk DeLuna gave twenty-three-year-old Suzanne Cardosa and his four children to twenty-two-year-old Paco. He told him to take care of them, make them his family.

# 3

## May 9, 2004

The moneyed class and rich Europeans, a number of whom are older French widows, live along Boa Viagem. Their glistening white condominium buildings face east overlooking the beaches of Recife.

The poor live four streets back from the beach in the squalor of windowless public housing. When breezes die down, the flies come, attracted to the garbage flung out of the open ports where windows normally fit. A poor woman leans on one of the ports looking toward the ocean for a breeze, looking at where the moneyed class lives, wondering if it is possible for her to move four blocks closer.

Then this woman glances down from her fifth story port to the houses in the space between the rich and her; that is the next step up the ladder, middle class housing. In the second and third streets from the beach are smaller apartment houses, even a few private homes.

It is five thirty in the morning as she swats a fly away from her face and she notices a man emerge from one of the private houses below. He is short and powerfully built. He stretches outside of his home and begins an easy jog to the intersection, and he turns left towards the ocean. She loses sight of him and turns to begin her work day.

The man running takes less than a minute to reach the beach on his run. Chunk DeLuna begins every day this way. He knows he must remain strong. He knows his verbal ferocity must be backed up occasionally by physical violence. It is his way of life. What elevated him from homeless loneliness was his brute strength. It enabled him to become leader of his gang, and it enabled him to stay as leader. What came naturally to him was not the brute he had become, but his loyalty to those in his gang and those who helped him. While he is tough on his gang's members, they know he will defend them at any cost. He takes a good share of proceeds from the gang's work for himself, but he is generous to his boys. They would say he is firm but fair.

On this day like so many others just under the equator, the sun will heat the earth's air to one hundred degrees. It is the reason he runs early; already it is eighty degrees. This is also the reason the beach is full of tanned, healthy Recifians walking and swimming before 6 a.m.

There is no wind, only a gentle breeze right on the water at this hour. The water is flat, and as waves move toward shore they do not so much break as they rise, they just fall. There is no energy in the water, just calm, and perfect for the hundreds of swimmers early in before the workday begins.

Chunk sees the girl playing paddle ball with a young man as she does three or four days every week. The first thing he notices is her bare ass. There is a thong running through it and her ass is round and firm and glistens on the left cheek as the sun, just coming over the edge of the water, hits it. And as he does every time he passes by, he says, "Ola." The boy and the girl call back to him.

This day Chunk does something different—he stops. He finds this girl alluring. Her hair is pulled back tightly. She is several inches taller than Chunk, and the young man with her is several inches taller than her. She is pretty, not beautiful. She has a strong face that shows the mixed race of so many Brazilians. Her body is taut, tight as a drum, abdominal muscles with skin stretched across them, calves with muscles, thighs with a slightly bulging main muscle on the outside of each leg. Her arms are firm but not thin.

She stops playing and looks at the short stranger who always says hello but has never stopped before.

"Do we know you?" she asks with attitude and a smile.

"I'm Chunk, and I'd like to have a date with you," DeLuna says, now looking at the young man, daring him to speak.

"Why are you looking at him," she says. "Do you want to date him?" and she laughs, a mocking laugh, and her brother laughs with her.

Chunk smiles and says, "No," and he looks at her and adds, "I mean no offense to him."

The young man smiles. "There is no offense. Lupe is my sister. But who are you to just ask her for a date? We don't know you."

"Well, I say ola to you every morning. I see you out here, and I feel like I know you."

At that Lupe finds herself thinking, "I have seen this man in the neighborhood, heard of this man's reputation." She is correct; he is known in the area as the leader of a tough gang of thieves and drug dealers. She thinks he seems friendly enough even though he is hard to look at.

"Just because you say ola does not mean I know you," Lupe says. "The only way you can get to know me better is on a date, so yes, I will go on a date with you. When?"

Lupe Montserrat's brother, Jorge, is shocked. He also knows of Chunk DeLuna and does not think he is a good choice for Lupe. But he says nothing. He knows more of DeLuna's reputation than Lupe, and DeLuna is the type of man you do not anger.

Chunk smiles broadly, two gold teeth visible where once the canines had been.

Chunk DeLuna does not so much make love as ravishes a girl. This was among his earliest acts of violence. Whatever he wanted he took, usually at night, usually under the piers where girls would come around. That was where the boys of Chunk's gang were; a perfect lure for unsuspecting girls searching for love and finding horror in the form of Chunk DeLuna. If a girl resisted once Chunk began making his form of love, she could easily be punched into submission.

It was a different Chunk who took Lupe to Olinda Churrascaria, a steak restaurant at the water's edge in the ancient town of Olinda just north of Recife. As waiters carved slices of beef at the table and brought skewers of shrimp, Lupe was aglow. She had never been to a restaurant like this.

Later Chunk took Lupe to his home. She liked what she saw there; DeLuna had so much. Lupe's family was just out of the projects but had not moved into the middle class streets. They began back further, seven streets from the ocean with a small apartment. The Montserrat's had four rooms, with windows, that housed her parents, her older brother and two younger sisters. Chunk had seven rooms all to himself.

"This is nice," she said to DeLuna, looking around at the furniture, large leafed plants and colorful posters on the walls.

"Thanks. Let me show you something else that's nice," and he unzipped his fly and approached her.

"Is this the way you want me to think of you? As a crude pig?" she asked.

DeLuna froze, rage rose up quickly.

"Do you want to make love to me?" Lupe asked the volcano.

"Yes," he said, his hand emerging from inside his pants, relatively disarmed by Lupe's frankness.

"Show me your bedroom," she said with authority. "I am not some tramp for you to screw with. If we are going to make love, we will do it right or not at all."

Chunk nodded. No girl or woman had ever talked to him this way. He walked to the bedroom, and Lupe followed. And Lupe showed Chunk how to make love. She taught him to gently run his hand over her body. She put her arms around his back; it was wide and had no softness to it. She let him hold her round firm ass as he kissed her neck. When he started to suck on her neck she pulled back and slapped him in the face.

DeLuna sat up, enraged, and he raised his arm back to fracture her teeth.

"You touch me," she yelled in his face, "and you'll never touch this body again and you'll never know what heaven is like."

That night she broke him. He became tame, but only for her. And that same week she moved in with him. Chunk DeLuna was twenty-two and had found a soft side to himself. Lupe Montserrat was two months past her sixteenth birthday.

# 4

Chunk DeLuna had a theory of business; to him, it was a simple formula: physical strength and ruthlessness combined with understanding what business you were in. He was twenty-three years old when his theory of business began crystalizing.

"Carlos, time is important also. At thirty years old, we do not want to be having girls turning out tricks on the beach. Members of our gang can do that. Our work, yours and mine, will be different. We have our robberies, shakedowns, the prostitutes, and the drugs. The gang can handle these. We need to focus on our customers. Many of them have money, but they also have something else we don't—influence. These guys make decisions, they run businesses, they're in government. They like to gamble. We need to add gambling."

Carlos listened, partially. He was concerned about a phone call he received from Raphael who said the police had picked him up for pimping. Rule one with DeLuna was no arrests. He had not told Chunk about Raphael's call and was deciding how he should broach it. Carlos' brain was multiplexing as he thought about the grilling he'd given Raphael on what the police wanted with him. He learned that Raphael had given them nothing, but the police wanted to use him to infiltrate DeLuna's gang. He told Raphael to tell no one else about what occurred. And while Raphael was part of the larger DeLuna gang, his first boss was Carlos. Among the original four—

Carlos, Raphael, Pedro, and Paco—they were still a gang. A gang within the larger DeLuna gang. This attempt at infiltration bothered Carlos. It meant that the gang was now on the radar of the police—no longer seen as petty thieves but viewed as a larger criminal enterprise. He needed to think this through. He was sure he would not tell Chunk, who might see the attempt to get at Raphael as a chink in the armor, which might need to be eliminated.

"CARLOS!" DeLuna screamed, "Did you hear what I said?" the demanding DeLuna inquired. It was a trait of DeLuna's to scream at someone he believed was ignoring him. It was an insecurity. He needed to matter; he needed to be heard.

"Yes, Chunk, I heard what you said," the tall man replied. What was also occurring in Carlos' mind was a matrix. What Chunk said made sense, but Carlos was seeing something else.

"Chunk, we have these separate units where Raphael runs the girls and Pablo and Pedro the drugs. Our customers are buying the girls, buying the drugs—the same customers. Some customers for drugs go somewhere else for girls. They should be coming to us for everything: girls, drugs, gambling. We should service them across these "businesses.""

"You were listening," DeLuna smiled. "That's it; that's our business—service. If you want it, we have it," DeLuna jumped in his seat.

"We need someone that goes across these units of ours. Someone who can see the whole picture," Carlos enthused. Carlos was why Chunk was successful. He had a big brain while DeLuna had the fierce muscle.

"You," DeLuna jumped again. "You're who we need doing that. You get it, Carlos. I need you to figure this out."

And Carlos and Chunk did figure it out. By the time DeLuna was thirty, there were units that specialized: girls, drugs, shakedowns, and gambling. Using shakedowns of politicians and government agencies that issued permits, the gang managed to get two casinos opened—one in south Recife and one in Olinda. Carlos started keeping written records and files on every customer. Carlos automated the files, which had information on who was using all of their services and how many times. If the client had a drug problem, Carlos made sure that customer had a prostitute and a gambling debt. The business was full service—you used one part of it, you used the full service.

One particular client was out on a ledge. He was a director of contracts for Purnambuco state, the northeast state of Brazil that encompassed many of DeLuna's criminal enterprises. Silvio Morales could not get enough cocaine, and after a while, he was moved up to heroin. Once there, he graduated to the higher-end prostitutes. He was also given a large draw at DeLuna's casino in Olinda. Carlos could see it. He could have anything he wanted from Morales. He owned Morales and his soul.

One evening Morales had reached his limit in the casino. He was strung out on drugs and wanted more of everything. When the floor manager accompanied Morales to Carlos' office and presented the issue to Carlos, it then hit him. Carlos stood up, "You two wait here; I'll be right back." Carlos walked from his own office to DeLuna's, which was across the hall in the rear of the Olinda casino.

After a brief update on Morales and his situation, Carlos said, "Chunk, there's something more here. Morales owes 600,000 reals. He can't pay and is asking us what do we want. He wants to raise his limit and also get more H."

"Let's talk with him," DeLuna said rising and accompanying Carlos back across the hallway.

"Mr. DeLuna," the state director greeted Chunk with an embrace.

"My friend," DeLuna said, then freeing himself from the embrace that pulled him into the man's chest, stated, "Carlos tells me you need an extension of credit, a larger draw. Yes?"

Morales nodded.

"Which I am only too happy to provide," DeLuna continued.

A smile crossed the face of the man on a drunken high.

"But I need a little assurance."

"Yes, of course."

"How will you settle your account with me? It is now quite high, and you are asking to extend it quite a bit further," DeLuna said, then asked, "You know with the credit extension it will be 800,000 reals. How much do you earn a year, Silvio?"

"One hundred and sixty thousand reals," the indebted man demurred. "Look, what I can pay you with is worth more than money."

DeLuna, who kept money in US dollars in US banks in Brazil, converted the 160,000 reals in his head. ("$40,000 yearly, he owes me five years pay.")

DeLuna laughed, a crazy crooked smile came across his face, "Silvio, my friend, nothing is worth more than money."

"A government contract is. It keeps paying and paying," Morales offered confidently.

"What kind of government contract," Carlos asked.

"Cement. It's the new gold of Brazil."

"Make sense," DeLuna tightened up, not quite following where Morales was leading.

"My business is director of construction. I put out for bid all building contracts in the state of Pernambuco."

"And," DeLuna said impatiently.

"We are building our country anew with the new oil revenues. The oil flows, the cement pours, the money gushes out. It's all about cement."

"Cement, oil—get to it," DeLuna growled.

"The oil means nothing. But cement is letting us build Brazil."

"I don't have any cement; how does that help me?" DeLuna continued the chess match.

"But if you did have a construction business or a cement company, I could direct sizable multimillion real contracts your way."

Chunks body language was not positive. His head was swiveling; his feet were moving. Carlos on the other hand started smiling; a light had gone on. "I think I'll be able to figure something out," Carlos said. "I will work the details out with you," he concluded handing Morales a note for an additional fifty thousand credit for the night.

"Thank you, my friend," Morales slurred. "I will not disappoint you."

After Morales left Carlos' office, DeLuna exploded, "You gave him another fifty thousand credit without a plan to pay it back," he screamed, "What are you thinking?"

"What you pay me for, exactly—thinking," Carlos shot back. "Morales may not have a plan, but I think I have one for him. We have many clients in our debt. One happens to be a cement manufacturer. He is about to have new partners—us."

DeLuna's primitive brain was following, although much more slowly than the ideas coming from Carlos.

"Chunk, this is it. This is our dream; a chance to get a legitimate front, to expand into government. To put all of this cross unit stuff—dependency, debt, background information—to good use. We've been playing for peanuts. What Silvio has is serious money. We can get out of the low end of the business, stop the petty robberies along the beach, and stop the shakedowns of the vendors. We can take the business up a notch, maybe even become totally legitimate. At least, we can appear that way."

DeLuna frowned. Not upset with Carlos any longer but with his own limited ability to see that the theory of the business they were in was evolving to something he could grasp but not as fast as he knew he should. He was upset that Carlos was that much smarter than he was. In the end, he calmed himself knowing that Carlos would not be at this point but for him. For all he knew, Carlos would still be diving off the bridge with Pedro, Paco and Raphael along with the dog. Therein lay the theory of business, mutual dependence—DeLuna's muscle and Carlos' brain. Those would be the keys to running their business across a platform of crime underpinned by drugs, prostitution, gambling and institutional corruption encased in cement.

*********

When Mercosur, the South American free trade treaty, was passed, it promised to open a new era of regional growth for all Latin American companies. One export from Argentina and Mexico that quickly found new markets in Brazil was cement. Brazil was going through a great growth spurt, and construction was leading that boom.

Cement exporters from Argentina and the giant Mexican cement company, Cemex, were posing new problems, more complex than Brazilian cement manufacturers had ever encountered.

These foreign exporters would offer the cement at a very good price but would seek to horizontally integrate themselves into the builders by offering a full supply chain: delivering the cement to the site, mixed in their own trucks, they would frame and block the targeted areas, such as foundations or ascending floors. They would do this all for the same price as bags of cement of the Brazilian cement companies, who did not have the value-add of the supply chain.

However, the cement company Chunk and Carlos wanted to acquire was the opportunity to give the members of the gang a new face; and while still nowhere near as profitable as drugs, it held promise for the future. As his client, Silvio Morales, the director of construction permitting for the State of Pernambuco, told DeLuna, with a cement company, Morales would be able to direct contracts for cement to him. So Chunk bought the cement company for several million dollars; most of which was obtained in fraudulent loans provided by a banker client of DeLuna's who was drug-dependent and heavily in debt to him.

Chunk changed the name of the cement company to CDL Cement; he liked having his initials public. He later added CDL Enterprisa as the formal title of the company, noting that there were other businesses besides cement, but none he would identify in public. CDL Cement was significant in size but significantly unprofitable and could not compete. It had professional managers running the company, and DeLuna's presence was to be more of a silent partner. The competition continued to heat up, and as losses grew, Chunk became less silent.

CDL Cement's president, a middle aged man by the name of Ignacio Braun, had been a general manager for one of the divisions of the company. After assuming ownership, Chunk met with Ignacio and the chief financial officer. He described what he expected from the company, offered the job of president to Ignacio, who asked Chunk "what about the current president, Juan Lopez."

"Mr. Lopez has a new assignment—retirement. What other questions do you have for me?"

He had none. He accepted the job, and unfortunately, he accepted Chunk's terms. Carlos drew up the terms: 20 percent revenue growth and 15 percent net profit. Chunk expected this from a company with 5 percent gross margins that was losing one million dollars on twenty million dollars of sales. The problem for Ignacio would be the way the new company would deal with missed expectations; it would not be a lower performance review, a missed bonus or even a firing. It would be far more personal.

Chunk along with Carlos, who was overseeing other businesses, would meet with Ignacio and the chief financial officer monthly to review the progress of the cement business.

Sadly, for them and their immediate successors, progress was not fast enough. Newspapers reported it strange that two presidents of the CDL Cement company had met violent deaths.

The third time was a charm for DeLuna. He installed Carlos as president along with a new chief financial officer. During the course of the three years that DeLuna and Carlos had been micromanaging, Carlos actually learned quite a bit about the cement business, plumbing its depth with rigorous questioning of everyone in and out of leadership positions. Carlos, in fact, had become quite popular inside the company with midlevel managers. He had risen from the shadows where he had been assigned by Chunk as a special assistant to Ignacio and then to later succeed his dead predecessors.

Together with the company's larcenous sales vice president, Carlos put a plan in place to lock out the foreign competition since local competition had been dealt with already. Each state in northern Brazil had a director of construction permitting—no permit for a site, no building. Through a series of relationship-building experiences with these gentlemen to some of the bordellos in Raphael's division of CDL, Carlos treated the state executives like royalty. Plenty of cash changed hands funded from the drug operations.

Now developers were willing to pay a higher price for CDL cement since dealing with CDL always made the permitting process easier, especially when the state directors could see a signed contract between the developer and CDL, where CDL was the cement provider and or site contractor. Each state director of construction permitting was given a significant bonus for every approved permit that carried a CDL contract.

Carlos' sales director for CDL felt like his sales force had been significantly expanded. Building developers were now making sure that every application for a building permit included CDL since state directors were only awarding permits to CDL tie-ins.

The price rose on cement, and CDL learned some of the lessons of horizontal integration. It was now selling extended services at much higher prices than those of the Mercosur players, who surprisingly just could not compete with CDL.

Additionally, bribery of bankers and public officials became common as the gang gave them kickbacks on construction projects they funded, in the case of banks, or approved, in the case of additional permits required from public officials.

Chunk, the homeless boy on the beach, had become a murderous menace, but he now had a legitimate business front. He was contemptuous of men; with women he could be charming. The madness that was his behavior grew worse as he got older. It was as if all men, but for those in his enterprise, were competitors and needed to be eliminated.

However, he was always respectful of customers or those who could help him.

The doctor, the good doctor for one. And as the years passed, the respected included the politicians, the state directors of construction permitting, and the builders who were using his cement. He was respectful of them as long as they did what he wanted.

# 5

There is that age, somewhere between twenty-eight and thirty-six, when all the power in the world flows through a person of education and experience. A man who is learned in his field, one who has spent years in apprenticeship gathering knowledge and applying it to real world tasks, a man like this is powerful and respected. Chunk DeLuna is that man. Now thirty-one, he had spent years building his Rei de Praia, his gang of beach kings. And while still a crime problem in the beach areas, the gang had spread north to Olinda and all the way south, from the state of Purnambuco to the state of Bahia and its capital of Salvador. The gang multiplied like fishes and loaves; whereas it began with five, it now numbered over two hundred. Chunk had changed the gang's name from the youthful beach kings to the more reflective CDL Enterprisa.

CDL had many sources of income for this enterprise. The members began with petty larceny and occasional armed robbery. They moved up to dealing drugs for a Columbian. They expanded into prostitution and loan sharking. DeLuna became increasingly obsessive about his "businesses" as he now called them. However, Chunk found that no matter what business he operated there was always competition. It didn't matter if it was a San Salvadoran drug dealer encroaching on his territories or a Mexican cement producer trying to undercut his prices. The problems were the same; the solutions were the same.

And these problems came up frequently. For one such problem, Chunk called a meeting at his seaside villa in Recife concerning an out-of-town drug dealer encroaching in Olinda and Recife. Chunk got a report from Paco who ran that portion of the business for the gang. It was an important meeting since Chunk's Columbian supplier was there with his complaints; in fact, he began the meeting.

"You guys have got to fix this. These blackies from Salvador are stealing your business, and when they are stealing your business, they are stealing mine also. They don't buy from my cartel but from one of the others. We're losing out here," Roberto Calo told the six men present.

Carlos chimed in, "Drugs are the key to everything, Chunk. If we don't have drugs, we don't have all the cement tie-ups. The drugs are the key to everything in our cross business units."

Angel Pagan, a boyhood friend of DeLuna's from San Blas, Puerto Rico, had joined the gang several years earlier and was one of its leaders. Pagan's business was eliminating the competition. And while Chunk DeLuna was vicious, even DeLuna was wary of the sadistic Angel Pagan and the extent he would go to inflict pain on an enemy. In fact, the only reason that the beach kings ever had competition was due to new entries into the marketplace. Experienced dealers left Chunk's business alone; you just did not want to suffer the consequences.

"So, Paco," Pagan began, "do you know these guys Roberto is talking about.

"Yes, we have talked about this before. It wasn't a big deal till now," Paco said. "But when they start threatening our street-level guys and putting themselves in our buildings to deal, like we're not even there, well, that's enough. Yes, we do need to act."

"You give me the locations, every location where this is happening, and I will take care of it." Pagan said.

Over the next several days, Paco's dealers in and around Recife and Olinda funneled into Paco six main locations where the selling was going on. Some of Paco's men followed their competitors, and there was also a seventh location where three of the six dealers had gone, most likely a drug factory. Paco figured it was processing, cutting, and packaging the product as it arrived in from Columbia.

A second meeting was called after this information was gathered to decide how to approach the competition. Chunk, Paco, Angel, and Roberto the Columbian attended, which was again held at Chunk's stucco villa by the water.

"This is what we have so far," Paco proceeded to explain the details of the comings and goings of the encroachers. "Do you need more?"

"You did good, Paco," the Columbian said, "Now, Chunk, go kill them."

This interjection was inappropriate. The Columbian knew it, and Chunk got hot. But he decided to let the slight pass. It only mattered that Chunk knew this was his house and his gang and that he, Chunk, not some greasy colom-ball, as Chunk derisively referred to the Columbian when he wasn't there, would handle his own affairs, without any interference.

"Good job, Paco, that's enough for us to go on." DeLuna started, "How do you want to handle it, Angel?"

"I like the idea of the one central place to take out everything at once. From what you have given us, Paco, my guess is your guys did not identify anyone as a leader?" Pagan asked.

"No, except on two of the three times they ended up at the seventh location, in Olinda, my boys said a tall African came outside with the dealers who had gone in."

"OK, sounds like it could be from Salvador or from the south side of Recife, where more Africans live," Pagan said, continuing: "Paco, I want one of the guys who went to the seventh house to come with me. Give him all the locations, a description of the dealers, and have him pick me up at my place tomorrow night. We'll drive through the whole thing and see how it looks." Then looking at Chunk, Pagan said, "Then I will make a plan, Chunk, and bring it to you."

"I want to see this plan also," the Columbian said.

"I assure you, you will, Roberto," Chunk replied, deciding in that moment that whatever plan was developed, Roberto Calo could

46

go along for the ride and see first-hand what this gang could do when it applied itself.

Northeast Brazil was discovered and claimed for the king of Portugal by Pedro Alvares Cabral on April 22, 1500, with a fleet of thirteen ships and more than a thousand men. Olinda was a strategic town on the hill in this territory and settled in the 1500s by Portuguese who exported sugarcane and indigenous slaves. The original Portuguese occupiers were rivals of Dutch invaders who burned Olinda to the ground. While Recife and Olinda were also equatorial rivals early on, not much has changed in Olinda over the past four hundred years. It was rebuilt in the 1700s and retains much of its colonial charm.

In the colorful blue stucco home at 23 Predente de Morais Street, lived a Salvadoran by the name of Eduardo. Angel Pagan's men found that the occupant had lived there for about three months. Neighbors noticed men and women coming frequently to the home. The area was residential; the streets still cobblestoned. It was one of the main routes of the carnival procession proceeding lent, a rite, smaller by far than Rio, but no less spirited.

Angel considered the location. Some of Recife's business leaders made their homes here in the large colonial manors by the Sao Pedro Catholic church. It would be a problem with noise if they were to swarm into the narrow street, three cars filled with his men, busting open the door and blasting away the competition. Angel learned that the dealers came in the afternoon to drop off the day's proceeds and to pick up a drug supply for the next day. There would be too many neighbors in the afternoon when most of the dealers were there. It would be quieter later, but there would be fewer of Eduardo's dealers there. He would have to involve more of his men—stake out all seven locations and strike at the same time to stop alerts.

This was the plan he presented to Chunk, Paco, and Roberto Calo, the Columbian.

Chunk would personally do the work at the Olinda house, and Roberto and Paco would accompany him there. The attack would take place in two days using semi-automatic pistols; it would take place at 6 p.m. when many people were still on their way home from work or the beaches. It would be easier for one car with two or three men to leave any one of the seven areas and get into the flow of evening traffic; and given that they would only be taking out one or two people in each location, quicker with less chance of a prolonged gun battle.

On the second day, at 5:45 p.m., Chunk, Paco, and Roberto parked half a block away from 23 Predente de Morais, on a side street with the car pointed south, down the hill. The sun was still on the horizon; there was still plenty of sunlight. Chunk sent Paco to the rear of the building.

Chunk and Roberto drew their pistols from under their shirts. A car approached, and they quickly dropped them to their sides until it passed. Chunk stepped up on the one front stair to the door and tried the knob. It was locked. He looked at Roberto who raised his left hand in a knocking gesture. Chunk shook his head no.

The door was weather beaten, not thin but not strong. Chunk figured he could lean into it, break it open and made the motion to Roberto, who shook his head no. In that instant, Roberto knocked loudly. Chunk stepped back, ran at the door and broke it open. A small room to the right had two mattresses and no one in it. He kept running down the hallway; he heard voices as he burst into what was the kitchen. One man reached for his gun when Chunk shot him dead. Two others were behind the dead man, and Chunk shot them. A fourth man came in from another room behind Chunk. He had a knife, and as Chunk swung around, this taller fourth man slashed at Chunk. Chunk avoided the knife by stepping back. He looked at the man for a second and said, "Never bring a knife to a gun fight," and he shot him dead.

A fifth man, the Salvadoran, went out the back door. There were three shots; sounded like two guns, Chunk thought, as he ran out the back door. The Salvadoran was on the ground with a gun in his hand, raising it up. Chunk was turning toward him. A shot rang out, and the Salvadoran fell dead. Paco, who was on the ground bleeding with a leg wound, had fired just as the Salvadoran had DeLuna in his gun's sights.

"Nice shot, Skinny," DeLuna smiled at Paco. "Roberto help me," Chunk called to Roberto who came out and was now beside him as he lifted Paco up. "We'll carry him to the car and do a tourniquet there."

Paco said, "You gotta stop the bleeding now. It looks bad, Chunk."

"Shut up or it's gonna look a lot worse. You'll live," Chunk said as he and Roberto Calo placed Paco's arms around their necks and carried him back through the house.

There was a large duffel bag on the floor. There were several one kilo bags of cocaine in various stages of being cut and packaged for retail sales. There were piles of money on the counter by the sink.

"Hold him up for a moment," Chunk said, and he grabbed the bag, swept the money off the counter into it, then picked up the bags of cocaine and placed them in the bag. The open ones spilt the white powder over the bag and the money. Chunk then swung the bag over his shoulder. He replaced Paco's arm around his neck.

They walked out the front door as a car passed by with music blasting and the driver in a trance. They carried Paco around the corner to the car and laid him down in the back seat. Chunk tore off part of his tee shirt and put it into the bullet hole. Paco screamed. "Be quiet, you yell like a girl," Chunk said with a smile, and he laughed. Through his pain, Paco smiled.

Then Chunk took off his belt and wrapped it around the leg placing the end of it in Paco's hand. "Hold this and keep it tight. It will stop the bleeding till we get you to the doctor."

They drove over the cobblestoned streets with Paco reeling in pain with each bump.

Then they were down the hill, onto the beach highway back toward Recife in less than a minute—no police.

"You can't take me to a hospital with a gunshot, Chunk," Paco said, adding, "They'll call the cops."

"I have my own doctor. You just relax," and in ten minutes, they were crossing the bridge over the Capibaribe River. "Paco, you fool, look," Chunk said, as he pointed to three boys diving off the bridge into the river."

"I must be dying," Paco said, half laughing, half crying as he too remembered how he first met Chunk.

"It's a sign from God. You will be fine."

Roberto Calo was silent but impressed with the fearlessness of his business partner and his loyalty to his men.

In another five minutes, Chunk pulled up to a private home in the Derby neighborhood. He told Roberto to look after Paco; he would be right back.

Chunk knocked on the front door of the pink stucco villa with the green tiled roof. A maid answered, and Chunk said something to her. She went away and shortly a man appeared. Paco recognized him; it was the doctor from the hospital many years before who had saved Raphael's eye.

Chunk spoke with the doctor for a moment. He indicated to Chunk to pull the car into the driveway to the left of the house and to the back, which he did.

The doctor never said a word. He helped Paco out of the car. Chunk and Calo carried him into a small office that the doctor used as a home examining room. They placed Paco on the table. He leaned back and passed out from loss of blood.

The doctor pulled Paco's pants off, leaving him naked from the waist down. He pulled the belt off and pulled the wad of tee shirt out of the bullet hole. It had stopped bleeding. "Ok, let me work," and he indicated to Calo and Chunk they should wait outside. The doctor washed his hands rapidly, and as they started to leave the office, he put an instrument bag onto the table.

"Chunk, come back; I can use your help. I need you to hold onto him in case he wakes up. I don't have any anesthesia to give him," the doctor said as he was already prying his way into Paco's thigh with an instrument looking for the bullet.

Paco winced in his coma as the pain increased.

After two minutes of prying, the doctor found the bullet and removed it. He cleaned the wound and put several stitches inside the leg and several more into the outer skin.

"Chunk, I can't do much more for him here. He needs to be in a hospital and may need a transfusion," the doctor said, sweating, looking at DeLuna.

"Ain't going to happen, Doc," Chunk said as he pulled Paco's pants back on him. "You need to tell me what I need to do to help him recover in his house. And I will need you to make a house call tomorrow."

"Sure, Chunk, I'll come by. The best thing right now is to get him into bed resting. He's going to need lots of liquids."

Calo, who stayed also, looked on. He found the relationship between respectable doctor and drug dealer fascinating—fascinating that a doctor would do Chunk's bidding so willingly.

They carried the now partly conscious Paco to Chunk's car and again laid him down in back.

The doctor carried out a small bag and handed it to Chunk. "Here's some more bandages and antiseptic. Change the bandage twice a day and put some of this on the wound. It will help prevent infection. Watch for a fever. If he gets bad, Chunk, you'll have to bring him into a hospital."

"Got it, Doc, thanks," and they drove off.

Over the next week, Paco did better. Chunk took him home to Suzanne, to the small but happy house they shared with five children; Suzanne and Paco having had a child of their own. Once Paco was situated in bed, he quickly fell asleep. Chunk and Suzanne stepped outside, out of earshot of the children. "Your man saved my life today," a chastened DeLuna said to Suzanne.

"He ends up being shot, you told me on the phone. And now you say he saved your life?" she said, more curious than questioning.

"We were dealing with some bad guys, but we took care of the job. The guy who shot Paco got the drop on me, but Paco finished him off," DeLuna turned and walked toward his Alfa Romeo, "One moment," he said over his shoulder. He opened the trunk and pulled out the large duffel bag he had taken from the Salvadoran's house earlier. He had taken the cocaine out and cleaned the bag up, leaving the money in it. Chunk placed the bag at Suzanne's feet unopened.

"This is for you and Paco and the kids." As he continued to talk, Suzanne bent down and unzipped the bag.

On seeing the amount of money, perhaps $200,000, she gasped.

"Paco and you are making a good life for those kids. He earned this today and since I asked him to help me out with you," DeLuna said looking her in the eyes. "He is doing a good job of taking care of all of you, isn't he," DeLuna stated; he was not asking. It was obvious from looking at the health of the children, the cleanliness of the home, and the happiness that was there.

"Yes, Chunk, he really is," she paused, questioning herself for what she wanted to say next but decided to push on. "I'm not too sorry it did not work out for us." DeLuna grunted in agreement. "But I am grateful that you were so smart to give me and the kids to Paco. He is a good father and husband." DeLuna smiled at both the compliment and the insult he felt from her last sentence.

"And now this, so much money!" Suzanne wrapped herself in a hug around DeLuna, and whispered in his ear, "If you need anything ... you know ..."

"Yes, stop, I understand. Thank you, but no. I have all I can handle with Lupe," he laughed. "She's an animal."

The doctor came by three of the first four days that Paco was at home. In this same time frame, Pedro, Paco's twin, took over his brother's part of the drug operation and filled Chunk in on the results of the attack on the rival dealers. Of the six other locations, four had just one person and Paco's men killed all of them. At one location, there were two men and a brief gun battle took place before Paco's men overwhelmed them and killed them. The sixth location was the only failure. One of Paco's men was killed, another wounded. There had been four men in the house—three were killed, the fourth got away. Paco's men were searching for him. They knew who he was, kidnapped his sister, and told his mother that if he didn't surrender they would cut his sister's head off.

On the fifth day, Chunk ordered it done. "Cut her head off and drop it off on the mother's front door. These people think we're playing with them. Leave a note under the head that if her son ever appears in Purnambuco we will kill her."

52

Pedro argued that the girl is only fifteen. "She didn't do anything. She doesn't know any of us and can't harm us."

"Pedro," Chunk began angrily, "you know better. No witnesses. Her brother knows what went down, knows who we are. If we let the sister go, he will see it as a sign of our weakness. It will only encourage him."

"But, Chunk?" Pedro pleaded.

"What's the matter with you? Have you gone weak on me? Look what they did to your poor brother. What they did to his men. What they tried to do to our business. No. Do it and don't question me again."

Pedro acknowledged Chunk's order.

Pedro was troubled; he did not sleep that night and arose soaking wet with sweat.

She was a kid, he told himself as he drove to the safe house where she was being held. When he got there, he entered the house, grabbed the girl, slit her throat, and when she was dead, he cut off her head. That night he left her head with the note at her mother's front door. Chunk's gang never had trouble from the Salvadorans again.

# 6

After she had been living with Chunk for some time, Lupe became aware that he had previously been with Paco's wife Suzanne and had fathered four of her five children. But she never got to know Suzanne. So it was on the occasion of one of Chunk's parties, where wives and girlfriends were invited, Lupe sought Suzanne out.

"I'm so happy that you could come tonight," Lupe greeted Suzanne in the entry foyer of her home. Paco spied Chunk in the salon where many of the party goers had gathered and left the ladies talking.

"You have a beautiful home," Suzanne said, without a trace of envy. Paco had told her of the magnificent waterfront mansion Chunk had built. The Chunk she knew never would have come this far. In her mind she saw Lupe as formidable, somehow able to aim "the beast," her term for DeLuna when talking with Paco. As was Paco's humble and loyal way, he would counsel Suzanne, "You can't talk about Chunk like that. He provides us a good life."

"Paco, it's only between us, and that is what he is."

"Not to us he's not."

Now standing here in Lupe's presence, she saw a difference between herself and Chunk's woman. Suzanne knew she was attractive with curves right where men like them, even after five children. Lupe was different, striking. She was tall for a young woman and fit. She looked strong.

"Let me get you something to drink," Lupe said, slipping her arm through Suzanne's. As they walked to the patio and the poolside bar set up for the evening, Suzanne felt something—not a chill, more a thrill. She felt something for Lupe, for the warmth Lupe was showing her, even though she had been a past lover of DeLuna.

They chatted as they got their drinks, small talk. Suzanne was admiring the evening, the setting. "Everything here fits; it all works so well together for the eyes."

"We are very fortunate," Lupe replied and then she observed the party moving noisily to the patio through the French doors of the salon. "It's quieter along the beach without all that crowd." She again slipped her arm through Suzanne's and said, "Walk with me."

Chunk saw the two women going off towards the beach along the wooden walkway over the shallow dunes. He wondered what they were up to.

Along the sand in the black night, Suzanne looked to the sky and exclaimed, "What is that."

Lupe looked up and saw the seam of a hundred billion stars across the sky, "It's our galaxy."

"Oh my God!" Suzanne cupped her mouth. "Those are stars?"

"Exactly, just like the sun."

"All this time right there and I've never seen it."

"I know. Living in the city, only a few miles away, all that light. It's different here," Lupe said in appreciation of what she had, what she knew she had, what so few young women her age would ever have.

"You said it, Lupe," Suzanne agreed, warming to her new friend. "It seems like Chunk has changed since he was with me. You must be good for him."

"Wellllll," Lupe said stringing out the last part of "well" long enough for both women to look at each other, then smile coyly at each other in the dim light, and then burst out laughing.

"I guess not," Suzanne said, and they laughed louder.

"I didn't know you two knew each other?" a loud voice said from the darkness.

The women jumped from the fright. It was Chunk, approaching them.

"Are you following us?" Lupe said sternly.

"Yes, I'm following you," DeLuna, now in their midst, said slurring his words. "Don't you know it's dangerous out here at night? There was a robbery on this beach only a week ago."

Probably one of your thugs, Lupe thought. "So, that's why you followed us?" Lupe was mad.

"Yes, why else would I follow my girls?"

"I'm not your girl any longer, Chunk," Suzanne said, emboldened by being with Lupe. She was also upset at having this quiet moment with Lupe interrupted. "Remember, you gave me away."

DeLuna stumbled forward and slapped Suzanne across the face with his left hand. She dropped her drink and raised a hand to her face. DeLuna pulled his right arm back ready to punch Suzanne. Lupe dropped her drink, stepped forward, and slapped DeLuna on his left cheek with her left hand. She got between Suzanne and Chunk and punched him in the temple with her right hand.

DeLuna screamed at her, "You bitch!" and pushed Suzanne aside as he prepared to pummel Lupe senseless.

"Come on, Chunk. Go ahead," Lupe taunted. "You touch me again, you can go to bed with Paco. Suzanne and me will become lovers," and she laughed as she put her arm around Suzanne.

Suzanne did not smile; she was too afraid of what she was seeing. But she knew she would always love this brave woman who was embracing her, for standing up for her, even as she now taunted "the beast."

DeLuna's eye blinked several times rapidly. What? He could not understand what Lupe was saying, doing. Yes, that was it. He had it right. She was taunting him. Telling him she'd deny him and become the lesbian lover of his former girlfriend.

"I'd like to see that," he said half laughing. "Go ahead; make love to her right here. I'll watch."

A bond occurred right then. It would last forever. Two women were seeing the exposed perverted mind of someone each of them had loved, or rather made love to, or rather endured what he did to them sexually.

DeLuna had accomplished in seconds what normally takes a lifetime—steeling two people in a friendship where each would do anything for the other. Anything.

Lupe with her arm around Suzanne's shoulder said, "Let's go off, away from this bad boy and make love in the sand." Both women began laughing hysterically, walking back to the party.

DeLuna fumed. "Fuck," he screamed loudly into the blackness, and the echo he heard back was the laughter of two friends fading from his sight.

"You bitches will pay," he said, woozy and wobbling as he skulked behind them.

\*\*\*\*\*\*\*\*\*

In the coming weeks and months, each woman embraced and relished that bond created on the beach.

Lupe took to driving the Audi A8 to Suzanne's house on hot afternoons and taking her and her children to the beach in Recife.

There were no recriminations from DeLuna for the beach incident. Lupe thought, maybe he was just drunk enough to have forgotten. Paco said something to Suzanne that suggested he had been dissed.

"Suzanne, what did you say to Chunk. He seemed upset that you and Lupe made fun of him somehow."

"Paco, nothing happened. Lupe and I were just getting to know each other and that crazy man snuck up on us along the beach. Scared the hell out of us in the dark." Nor did Suzanne tell Paco that DeLuna had slapped her. There was nothing Paco could or would do about that. Suzanne was alright with that though. Paco was a good father, a good husband. What he did away from home she knew vaguely and did not like it. But it provided a life for the seven of them, a happy life together.

On one particularly hot day at the beach but with a cool ocean breeze, Lupe lay on her side facing Suzanne, who was lying back on a blanket.

"But before me, before either of us, do you think he was like this?" Lupe asked.

"It has gotten worse; it gets worse," Suzanne answered. "He was just a baby, fourteen, when we met. Something happened in his life not too long before I met him. Made him very bitter. When I used to talk with him, I could see the good boy there, and then something inside him would override it, put the boy down. Something was making him mad and tough. He would never talk with me about it though."

"Yes, I can see there is something back, much further, since I didn't meet him until he was twenty-two. There is a lot of anger—not at me though. He is mostly tender. I think I help calm him. Occasionally though, I get it too: slaps, punches, kicks. I'm so close to it, I can't tell if it's getting worse."

"When Paco has his brother Pedro over and just the two of them are talking, I listen from the bedroom. The things they talk about, the violence Chunk does, not to them but to their enemies, it's sick. And as their gang gets bigger and bigger, the things they do, you just can't imagine. It scares both Paco and Pedro."

"Aren't they doing things with him?"

"No, they run the drug part of their business," Suzanne at thirty-four was saying to Lupe, realizing for the first time how young Lupe still was at twenty-six. "When it comes to the tough stuff, Chunk likes to do it himself or with Angel Pagan, his hommie from Puerto Rico."

"I know Angel. He seems nice. At least, he's always nice to me."

"Be careful," Suzanne warned. "He's the devil himself."

"No way," Lupe said, puzzled.

"Paco is really afraid of him. He's ten times meaner than Chunk. Stronger. Much more brutal."

"Like how?"

"No, Lupe. I can't even describe what I've heard," Suzanne said, trembling, tears welling up in her eyes.

Right then, three of Suzanne's children came back to the blanket, and she wrapped towels around them.

"Is Auntie Lupe making you cry," the youngest child asked.

"No," Suzanne said, now laughing. "I just got some sun tan lotion in it."

Lupe stood; all five feet nine inches and 120 pounds bound together by sun drenched bronze skin, covered barely in an orange bikini. A middle aged man walking by looked, passed, and turned back again to glimpse Lupe. She smiled brightly at him.

"Sweetheart," Lupe said, looking down at the oldest of Suzanne's children, "Would you watch your brothers and sisters while your mom and I go for a walk."

"Yes, Auntie," the girl replied politely.

The taller, younger woman and her shorter, older, but no less attractive, friend walked along the sand toward the retreating tide. Two teenage boys walked by, looked at the women and whistled.

"At least we know Chunk has good taste in women," Suzanne laughed.

"I hoped I could change him," Lupe began. "He had, he has good qualities. He cares for me; I know that. He's loyal to his stupid gang. He's very generous. He's always giving money away."

Suzanne smiled knowingly. "That is so funny you say that. I had the same idea. Change him. Then he would get so stubborn. He would lock into a place where I couldn't reach him. The longer we were together the more I realized I couldn't do it."

Lupe understood. Unsure how to broach this next topic, she began, "Suzanne, you and I are friends. Right?"

"Lupe, you know we are. What is it?"

"Please, don't be offended. I don't know how to ask."

"Lupe. Stop it. You can ask me anything. You know that. You're the only person in my life who has ever stuck up for me, you know, what you did with Chunk that night."

"That's funny. I just like putting him in his place. Besides, I'll not have him hitting my best friend. Me, OK, but not you."

A glow, an aura came over Suzanne. She had never, not since she was thirteen, had someone call her a best friend, and certainly not someone as strong, rich, and stunning as Lupe Monserrat.

Suzanne stopped walking. Lupe looked at her, and Suzanne stepped into Lupe and hugged her. She leaned her head on Lupe's shoulder and began to cry.

"Sweetie, what is it?" Lupe said, putting her hand on Suzanne's head and stroking it gently.

"I love you, Lupe. You are more kind and sweet than any person I have ever known. You make me feel joy in life. I have my kids and Paco. But I didn't have a friend. Now I have you."

"Ok, then," Lupe laughed putting her hand on Suzanne's shoulder. "I guess I can ask you anything."

They laughed, put their arms around each other's waists. Lupe grabbed an infinitesimal amount of fat on Suzanne's side and squeezed it. "Better lose this if you want the boys to continue whistling," then she pinched it. Suzanne squealed and slapped Lupe's nearly bare rear end.

"What I want to know," Lupe said as they turned and began walking back, "Is why Chunk let you have your kids. What I mean is, he won't let me have any."

Suzanne laughed, "That's almost funny. He didn't want any kids either. Did he ever talk about us, about me and the kids?"

"No."

"Never?"

"No."

"That makes sense." Suzanne paused. "You can't repeat what I'm going to tell you. He'd kill me."

"You know I wouldn't."

"I know. Then sit down." They sat down, and Suzanne proceeded to share the early version of life with Chunk: the part where he went to prison at fourteen and told her to kill their unborn baby; all the way up to the part where he gave her and the kids to Paco along with all the blood and bruises in between.

Lupe listened and tears formed in her eyes, ran down her cheeks. She wrapped an arm around Suzanne's shoulder.

"I'm OK, Lupe. I should be listening to you. I know it is worse."

"It is, but that's a story for another day at the beach."

Suzanne and Lupe looked at each other, tears of support, friendship, and love flowed down their cheeks. Sitting in the sand, in the afternoon breeze, they embraced.

*********

In the coming months, their friendship did grow. Auntie Lupe became closer to Suzanne's five children and their mother. Whenever Chunk was away, it was in Suzanne that Lupe sought solace. Suzanne's oldest daughter would watch the children when the friends went out for dinner or to a movie. They were united by the strongest bond imaginable—they knew the depths of depravity the other had been subjected to at the hands of the beast. For Suzanne it was arguments, never ending arguments, ending in beatings that grew worse as time passed. For Lupe, who was iron-willed, it was domination by a fierce wild man, however, she would never give in to his domination of her. She could take it; she fought back. When he hurt her, she made sure she hurt him. If not physically, she knew she could beat him emotionally, sexually. Denial was not a weapon; it was a response. And yet she always wondered why he was this way. Who made Chunk this way? She knew from the good things he did, the beast was not his true nature. What changed and continued to change him?

# 7

"He's not impossible to arrest," Captain Luis Garza of the Recife Police was saying.

"He is impossible," Oscar Omera one of his lieutenants replied. "We're establishing contact inside his gang. But arrest, right now? Impossible."

Captain Garza and Lieutenant Omera were arguing over the wire-tapped conversation they had been listening to between Chunk DeLuna and Suzanne Cardoso, Paco's wife.

"He said Cardoso's husband Paco killed the Salvadoran. What else are you looking for," Captain Garza said.

"Yes, he said the Salvadoran was about to kill him and Paco shot him first. That sounds like self-defense?"

"You sound like you're working for them. What the hell. Arrest DeLuna."

"And then what?" replied the lieutenant, Omera. "We arrest him, he gets bonded, and through all his corrupt influence he bribes judges, jurors and goes free."

"Lieutenant, not one more murder by this beast in our city. Figure it out; work with the Federal Police and the drug unit in Bahia where DeLuna has expanded. Do you understand?"

Exhausted from the debate, and after being reminded it was DeLuna who deposited the head of a young woman he had kidnapped on her mother's front door steps, Omera knew it was time to stop arguing. He did not like the order, but it was his unit's responsibility to quell crime in the northern Recife and Olinda district. The captain was right.

Omera had joined the force after university and move rapidly to lieutenant. The department was seeking more educated officers and moved them quickly through a series of assignments to challenge and broaden them. Omera was twenty-nine years old; his captain thought he might be moving too fast, unable to grasp how a low-life like DeLuna had grown powerful across the major crime units in his command including murder, drugs and prostitution. Bribery, extortion and fraud were in another command of the force, and they were having the same problems with DeLuna there.

The Chief of Recife's police force liked Omera for another reason. He had pull. Omera was from a middle class but well-connected family. When needed, his influence could counter the damage that Chunk DeLuna could do to the legal system. The appointment of Oscar Omera was a structured tactic to bring down Chunk DeLuna any way possible. Omera didn't yet realize his strategic importance in this chess match. Captain Luis Garza saw himself as a pawn in the middle of the chief's strategy. He was starting to think it was only a matter of time before Lieutenant Omera would take his job.

# PART

## 2

# 8

Brazil! At once exciting and exotic; rich and poor; ambitious and laconic. Beckoning the world to come. Bem-vindo! It is time. The world stage awaits, and the table is set. The Olympics! A showcase for the world to see. Rio, Amazonia, Brasilia, and Sao Paolo. Favellas, music, and Carnival. World class slums; first-class beaches. The beautiful people.

Seven hundred years ago native Indians owned the earth, the jungle and the beaches. Sugarloaf was merely a mountain; Christ had not yet come to the New World. Canoes plied the Amazon River, the River Negro; trade flourished between tribes. An empire existed. Now the world would come and see its oxygen plant, see the mighty Amazon, the watershed of a nation, visit exotic jungles, still see some of the native people as they existed seven hundred years ago. Even the city of Manaus, eighteen hundred miles from Rio and deep in the Amazon jungle, would showcase itself hosting Olympic events.

Brazillian oil, Rio Favellas, world admiration, relocating two hundred thousand poor, jubilation at the negotiations, and disgust at the reality.

The World Cup of Soccer in 2014 and the Summer Olympic Games in 2016 were coming to Brazil welcomed in a carnival-like outpouring in the streets in 2009. Forever, the Southern Hemisphere had been overlooked by the Northern's disdain for the third world. Finally, recognition of the arrival of the world's fifth largest country. Brazil was one of the BRICs, those constantly emerging economies of Brazil, Russia, India, and China, that could become financial powerhouses of the future through their national and human resources but never seemed to get there. Now though, now was Brazil's time!

Once the applications had been submitted and it became apparent Brazil was a strong contender for the Olympic games, contingent contracts were let out to build the enormous infrastructure that would support the events.

And prior to that, infrastructure ministers for each of the Brazilian states met as a group with the Brazilian Olympic Organizing Committee.

What was known from the beginning was that the Olympic Games would cost Brazil its fortune. While it was broadcast that operating costs for the Olympics would be offset by the revenue from worldwide TV and attendance at the venues, what was known but not broadcast was that the capital costs to build the Olympics and the infrastructure to support it would exceed $50 billion. The amount was so vast it would be suppressed at every level, but the political machine that pressed onward saw in its vision a two-fold benefit for Brazil—vast improvement in roads, the electric grid and public transportation, as well as world-wide recognition for Brazil's fabulous way of life.

"DPGC—that's the business model," Carlos was telling the meeting of the four "business unit" heads and Chunk DeLuna. "We will lead with drugs, the prostitution and gambling, and finally cement. Cement as we know holds everything together. Once we give the ministers and contractors DPG and they give us their cement business, we will be bound together. This is our strategy for the World Cup and the games."

Brothers Pedro and Paco had been jointly running the drug portion of CDL Enterprisa for several years, ever since Carlos had moved up to take over the cement business. And while Raphael had poor vision out of one eye, his eye for attractive women to join the prostitution business was very sharp.

The four boys that Chunk DeLuna beat up on a bridge years before were now joined with him in the largest criminal organization in Brazil. It was so large; it was invisible. Each of the elements were constructed of cells, where elements of one cell knew nothing about other cells above, below and beside them. The only place it came together was at the business unit level.

Pedro and Paco had been so good at compartmentalizing their drug operations that occasionally when one franchised cell would exceed their own territory and get into a shooting war with another, it would invariably be against one of the brothers' own cells. Pedro or Paco would enter the dispute and nudge the offending expander back into their own territory, usually offering them ideas how to grow their business within their own turf, not out of it.

It fell to Chunk and Carlos, on the other hand, to see where a horizontal advantage existed in a geographic area. In the background, Carlos had continued building an information warehouse with the help of key technologists in the IT department of CDL cement. This was not a physical warehouse for storing bags of cement, rather a data warehouse of important and influential people who were customers of multiple units of CDL. If a certain minister of construction was a cocaine user, it was important that he enjoy the other CDL products like women and gambling. It was important that compromising pictures from hidden cameras capture events of an evening and that gambling debts accumulated be bartered to the customer when influence was needed—say for a sign-off by a minister on a new contract or a waiver by a local contract administrator when a bid from CDL exceeded guidelines.

Over time the enterprise enveloped its prey like an octopus; multiple arms contributed to the electronic profile Carlos' unit maintained on all customers. The idea of the Five Rings Project, as the CDL Olympic initiative was known among the four business unit heads and DeLuna, was not some piece of brilliant criminal strategy developed by Chunk or Carlos. It was rather the desperation of a Bahia State procurement director of construction, Diego Negron, who brought the opportunity forward.

Negron, who two years earlier had been supportive of DeLuna getting three contracts in the city of Salvador in return for hefty bribes, had taken excess to a new level in his bravado to impress the provided high-end prostitute on his arm at the Salvadoran Palace, a new CDL casino. He took advances to cover his losses and at the end of a dizzying five-week spree of sex, drugs and gambling he owed the Palace three hundred thousand dollars, six times his annual salary.

Diego was brought before Carlos and Chunk and pled for forgiveness. Consequence is that place in your mind you hope never reveals itself; now he had to face the consequence of his wild behavior. He offered his services to aid Chunk and Carlos in some way. He explained that his duties for the state was granting permits and approving contracts, which Chunk knew from his earlier efforts for CDL, would now include two of the Olympic venues in Salvador. Carlos had been aware of Negron's state responsibilities but did not know of his new assignments for the Olympics.

In all the years they had known each other, Chunk and Carlos could look at each other and make a connection. Such a connection was made as Diego Negron explained his duties. After he left Carlos' office in the casino, DeLuna and Carlos were beside themselves with glee. They saw endless opportunities providing the cement, framing and even building the main venue, and they could provide the manpower from various unions they controlled.

"This is a model that can work in other states for us," Carlos offered. There were to be thirteen Olympic venues across Brazil that would host both the World Cup and the Olympic Games. "There are only two other companies with the cement resources that can do what we can," he later explained to Chunk and the other heads, Pablo, Paco and Raphael, as the Five Rings Project was born. "We have sixteen cement plants now and the back-up resources to build anything."

"We must act quickly," DeLuna added, "We must dominate in this new area."

"We'll be rich," Raphael replied.

DeLuna slapped Raphael's face, gently. "We're already rich," DeLuna chided.

"Then, now, we'll have everything!" the youngest of the five criminals laughed.

# 9

"Why are you so nasty?" Lupe said, adding, "Lately?" Although the longer she stayed with Chunk, the darker he became. Sure the animal who was quick to rage was always just beneath consciousness, but the beast had become more voracious, devouring its prey with no mercy.

What led to Lupe's decision to question DeLuna on this morning was his obsession to win new business and contracts for his cement company.

"Lupe, you don't understand the pressure I'm under. I've never had pressure like this before," he whimpered. "And now the unrest," he said referring to protests that had sprung up in some cities over the growing cost estimates of the World Cup and the Olympics.

Lupe had never seen him without his bravado, his pumped ego and puffed-up chest. Something was wrong. He was perspiring without movement.

That something had been accelerating for weeks. Yes, Brazil had bid for and won the rights to host the 2016 Olympics and the initial announcement triggered a national celebration of pride. No one was prouder than DeLuna. With his CDL Enterprisa, he was one of Brazil's leading cement manufacturers. CDL had fifteen plants up and down the east coast of Brazil and one inland at Manaus, positioning them perfectly to bid for and build several of the large Olympic venues.

The pressure DeLuna found himself under was a process that began with beating the competition to win bids to construct the stadiums and the Olympic villages. This would involve the use of all the political leeches doing his bidding to get CDL preferential treatment from state and district overseers. To enable sole source bidding that favored CDL would require clipping a few fingers when politicians balked.

The work Carlos, Raphael, the brothers Paco and Pedro undertook with their various elements of CDL, legal and illegal, had won them the rights to build six structures worth almost $1 billion. Getting the work was the core competence of CDL. You could not refuse to do business with them; you would did not want to face the consequences.

"La consequence, that is what gets contracts," Carlos was telling the now grown-up beach kings. "But, Chunk, are we overstretching ourselves? We've never built more than three structures at any one time."

"Buck up, weakling," DeLuna derided. "We've won the business, and we're going to build what we said we would build."

Lupe sat in on some of the "legitimate" business meetings, and she could see the weight of the enterprise pushing DeLuna down. He was a brute but not smart. He was clever but had no visceral feel for complexity.

Adding to the pressure on DeLuna was the fact that Lupe wanted children. She wanted a family; she was unfulfilled. Not that DeLuna didn't treat her well—she had more than she ever imagined, but DeLuna was unfulfilling.

The last time she had become pregnant the battle began again. "Just do it, Lupe. No discussion."

They had been together for ten years. She was twenty-six. She had three abortions and now Chunk wanted her to get a fourth.

"No."

She stood her ground for five seconds before DeLuna punched her in the temple, almost knocking her out. When she fell he straddled her and put his left hand on her throat. "You do it or else."

"Or else what," the defiant girl gurgled, swinging her legs wildly trying to break free.

"Or else I'll screw you to death," and he began tearing at her clothes. She fought, slapping at him, punching him, kicking him. Chunk smiled. He paused for a second in their battle, only a second, to admire the strength and fight of his woman, then he plunged into her.

For Lupe, sex was sometimes like this with him. It relieved him; it brought the fires down a few degrees. It made the world a little safer. And while she felt physically abused, she was strong, she could take it, and she knew he never meant to harm her. Occasionally, she found it thrilling.

On this particular occasion as they lay smoldering from the mighty blaze they had ignited, Lupe asked, "Why?"

"Lupe! Please stop."

"But why, you never explain yourself."

"Why? Because one day they're gonna come for us. And we're gonna have to run. And I don't want to be leaving some little kid on the beach by itself."

# 10

*News Brazil—All Media*

*Silvina Arancha*

*June 25, 2013*

*Manaus*

*Brazilians are not happy!*

*More than one million protesters took to the streets during the month of June. Their issues: the cost of the 2014 World Cup and the 2016 Olympic venues. The cost of the two events is exploding and is now expected to exceed $30 billion.*

*Spending on this scale is viewed by most of the populace as wasteful to the extreme. Government services like public housing, transportation and education will be the losers as the government now must start making choices for which projects can go forward.*

*The World Cup is expected to spend $3 billion for new and upgraded stadiums, one of which, Brasilia's Estadio National, is already considered a white elephant. It will be a seventy thousand seat venue, costing $700 million and is expected to have little use when the events are done.*

*Maracana Stadium, the home of Brazil's soccer gods and a national icon, underwent a several hundred-million-dollar makeover, but a May match between Brazil and England was cancelled when the stadium was ruled unsafe for play. (The decision was reversed just in time, no doubt to some pricey political hand wringing.)*

*Organizing groups for the protests claimed that needed public works infrastructure projects are getting short shrift. Needed road, rail and housing projects tied to the World Cup and the Olympics are much farther behind schedule than the Olympic venues, claim these protest organizers. One can only hope that Brazil recoups some of its lost gold in Olympic gold.*

**********

Manaus, the steamy capital of Amazonia, was once again vaulting to the top of the cultural world. Two centuries ago it was a glittering opera house imported into the jungle on the back of mother rubber that brought fame to Manaus. Now it is a giant on the horizon, a fifty-two thousand seat stadium for Manaus, one of thirteen Olympic venues, being built to host the 2016 Olympics.

For Manaus, whose forth division soccer team, Nacional, owned by one Chunk DeLuna, had drawn a high of 3,215 paid attendees for its biggest game ever against Curitiba. This would change its standing in Brazilian soccer, in Brazilian culture. The crowds that would be expected in the future would assure a steady rise to the top of Brazilian club soccer. It would bring new tourism to the interior.

Protestors, who screamed corruption over the cost of such far-flung pork projects, were shouted down by politicians every step of the way; especially belligerent with the protestors was the senator representing Manaus, the capital of the state of Amazonas. That Senate seat had been bought and paid for by none other than Mr. DeLuna. DeLuna even bought the Nacional soccer club team for a fraction of its value. The value lay in its future and the future of Brazil. As a legitimate level four soccer team, it could invest, compete and grow. Other teams that had made the investment saw their fortunes grow as attendance soared with each new star added to the roster, each new stadium built and each new TV contract signed in soccer-mad Brazil.

DeLuna's own private hell began another way. By deciding to bid on Olympic venues, he had bitten off more than he could chew, taking too big a bite and now his brain was being stretched. It was not that CDL needed the Olympics; their core businesses were running very well. The drug business continued to grow. Everyone was in line, and the suppliers and dealers were working well together. Prostitution was soaring. New brothels were opening in all regions of Brazil; CDL Enterprisa had also gone international with brothels in Buenos Aires, Mexico City, San Juan, and New York City. Gambling had made a big comeback after the great recession.

The cement business and the new supply chain offerings were doing well, too well. DeLuna desperately wanted to be respected by the whole of Brazil, not just the underside. He kept pushing Carlos to grow the business; this became increasingly possible now that the cement business was more than just cement. The added services provided to developers had put CDL in the top tier of companies that developers would do business with. Additionally, the interlocking relationships of his other businesses ensured he would get the right people in his pocket for project approvals and permitting. These state representatives who succumbed to gambling, prostitution and drugs were the path in for DeLuna.

While the Olympics presented special challenges, DeLuna saw them as the fastest way to legitimacy, helping build his country's showcase to the world. The challenges began early in the Olympic bidding process, years before the events would be held.

The senator from the Brazilian state of Pernambuco, DeLuna's home state, was on the National Olympic organizing committee. Osvaldo Ottero was to oversee the development of the venues as head of the senatorial financial oversight committee. Because Brazil was funding the Olympics from taxpayer revenues, the committee was responsible for confirming the candidate cities that would win the bidding for various locations around the country. The city of Manaus was a troubling one for him. Manaus had a strong local contingent pushing for it, and the area had a high native Amazonian population that would increase inclusiveness and benefit local employment for the constructions jobs it would provide. Later these venues would remain and encourage tourism. However, the city itself and the surrounding area did not have the population to support the proposed fifty-two thousand seat stadium that would need to be built to qualify as a venue for the proposed soccer events. The additional and quite visible problem Senator Ottero had in supporting the nomination of a stadium for Manaus was that the current stadium, which had seats for thirty thousand, had an average attendance of 345 paid attendees for a minor league soccer franchise.

On the other hand, Senator Ottero reasoned, a benefactor of his, Chunk DeLuna, was pushing very hard to have Manaus win this stadium bid. CDL Enterprisa had the only cement plant and broad construction capability within five hundred miles of Manaus, therefore assuring that if Manaus won, CDL would win. This was the most important project that CDL had ever bid on and the most necessary for it to win. DeLuna in his discussions with the agent of misery for his gang, Angel Pagan, decided they needed an ace up their sleeve to keep the Senator's feet to the fire so they kidnapped the youngest of his three daughters. There was no ransom demand; she just disappeared. DeLuna had her taken to a safe house deep into the Amazonian forest.

Of all the Olympic venues DeLuna was bidding on, he was most certain of winning Manaus. Not only did he have the cement plant and construction company nearby, but he owned local labor through control of three critical trade unions: cement masonry, electricians, and plumbers. Additionally, the processes for permitting in the state were controlled by a director who was deeply into debt with DeLuna through gambling. DeLuna also had the man hooked on heroin. DeLuna had told his team putting the bid together for Manaus, "It is the smallest of all the Olympic venues and the simplest. If we cannot win and do this, we are useless for Brazil."

His team was impressed by DeLuna's sudden national spirit, but there was not a soul in the country that was not caught up in Olympic fever.

As cost estimates for the combination 2014 World Cup and 2016 Olympics rose to the $50 billion level during the pre-bid process, many politicians felt they had no room for failure. Senator Ottero was caught in a vise. He knew who had his daughter; he knew she would be returned unharmed once DeLuna's CDL Enterprisa won the bid for Manaus. But the President of Brazil made an impassioned plea at one of the Olympic Organizing Committee meetings. "This is the coming-out party in the world for Brazil. We cannot fail: our country, our reputation and our future all depend on every one of you doing your utmost to select the very best vendors at the very lowest costs."

Senator Ottero knew he was in trouble. He expected just the opposite was possible with DeLuna—the very highest prices for lower quality work. Yet, he could not let his daughter stay in the beast's arms. He talked with DeLuna on several occasions after the President's plea. In the meantime, the general public was getting anxious as the projected costs of the Olympics were starting to get out in the press. There had been unrest in several favelas in Rio and Sao Paulo. The headlines of local papers were starting to fan flames, "Billions for the Olympics; Nothing for the Poor." Left leaning forces worked up a series of large demonstrations.

DeLuna was having nothing of what the Senator was proposing. "But, Chunk, if you come in under the umbrella of one of two very large construction outfits out of Rio, we're definitely in."

"What are you saying, Osvaldo?" a quickly steaming DeLuna said as they finished their dinner at the Ricky's, a swanky seaside favorite of the Senator's in Recife. "Are you telling me this is not a done deal, that we do not have the contract for Manaus?" DeLuna concluded, now leaning into the table towards the Senator.

"Chunk, I'm being squeezed from all sides. I think I'm going to explode. My daughter has been kidnapped, the President is putting new cost and quality measurements on all the Olympic sites, and you're coming at me too hard," Senator Ottero concluded, looking at DeLuna with pleading eyes. Underneath the eyes was murderous contempt. He should confront the little bastard. Right here, in front of everyone, scream at him, "What have you done with my daughter?" But of course he would not, could not. Not if he ever expected to see Eugenia again.

"You award those contracts to CDL," DeLuna demanded in a dead monotone. "You will not screw me out of this. We will not only have this contract but others, but this is the first and the one we are best prepared to do well. Do you understand me?"

The Senator did not understand this ugly little man sitting across from him, not at all. DeLuna did not play by the same rules as everyone else. You could never expect him to do the right thing, to accept political difficulties. Once he had his claws into you, he considered that you were part of his organization, there for him to do what he wished. There was no washing each other's hands. He was the emperor; you were the slave. And now to himself, the Senator expressed deep regret for ever buying into the DeLuna madness. Yes, he was just a local director of municipal services when he first stumbled into the DeLuna's prostitution den in Olinda. Yes, DeLuna had gone easy on his gambling debts. Yes, DeLuna had backed him in his campaign for mayor of Recife. And, yes, it had been the financial backing of DeLuna along with union support from CDL Enterprisa's extensive influence across the Pernambuco state that enabled his victory. But Osvaldo Ottero was a now senator of the country of Brazil. He had higher responsibilities. He was above all that; he needed to be above all that. "Don't I?" he asked himself as DeLuna anxiously awaited an answer.

"Do you understand me?" DeLuna repeated, now leaning forcefully into the table, knocking a water glass over.

"Yes, Chunk," the Senator gritted his teeth. "We understand each other."

\*\*\*\*\*\*\*\*\*

The Senator knew one day he would kill Chunk DeLuna. "I am not someone you fuck with," Oswaldo Ottero screamed at one of his senatorial staff in a false, outrageous bravado on learning his daughter had been murdered.

The headline, three days after the dinner with DeLuna and Ottero, read "Senator's daughter found dead in Manaus." The story

78

went on to describe her kidnapping ten days earlier that had been kept out of the papers as the police waited for a ransom demand from the kidnappers. The police indicated the ransom demand never came, and they speculated the criminals may have gotten into disagreement, panicked and killed the girl. The police report was gruesome in the details: most of the girl's body had been burned away by acid. She was identified by her face—her head was the only identifiable part of her body. "Her death was excruciatingly painful as you can imagine," the police spokesman said, the newspaper report concluded.

"Papi," an aide to the senator said. "How horrible for your beautiful girl."

"Aye, it was horrible for my baby," the man cried. And when the aide left, Senator Ottero pulled up the attachment to an e-mail he had received earlier and he watched again as the forty second video clip showed the death of his daughter. The film began as a backhoe extended its arm, lifted it and raised a chain that was connected to a metal cage. The camera had zoomed in close and a young girl could be seen in the cage, strapped upright to its steel frame. The arm of the backhoe swung the cage up and over a large round vat and was slowly lowering the cage into the vat. "No, no," shrieked the voice of the girl as the cage descended."

The Senator gripped his desk, his face screwed up into the torturous pain his baby was about to endure, "No, no," he moaned.

The camera angle rose up to follow the cage into the vat. The girl's screams were unearthly; horrifying as the acid first burned her skin. Then as the girl's arms swung in pain inside the cage pieces of flesh peeled off as the acid ate through her body, all the while lowering her, inch by inch, into the acid bath. The backhoe stopped lowering her at her neck. Finally, mercifully, the cries stopped. Later when the partial skeleton was found, only the head was identifiable. The message accompanying the e-mail into an account only he could access told the Senator to "playball or I'll roast your other two daughters the same way."

Senator Ottero was insane with grief. What type of monster would do this to an innocent child? Where could such evil come from? The pain he now felt was numbing. His life was over. Life, after seeing a child of yours murdered in such a horrible way, was not worth living.

Ottero knew who had done this. He would ensure DeLuna got the contracts to build the Olympic venue for Manaus. He would help him get other contracts. And he would wait. He would have DeLuna watched every second of every day until the time was right.

He knew DeLuna was trying to show his toughness and ruthlessness through acts of pure horror. When the world order dissolves, the senator thought to himself, the evil shown to civilization, by those who would undo it, will be incomprehensible. "I will find everyone close to DeLuna, and they will all get an acid bath. I will personally lower them, one at a time in front of DeLuna. Then lastly I will lower him, slowly as he begs for mercy. Until he begs to be put out of the misery, hanging from a chain by his hands and slowly dipped into that acid bath. I will watch as the acid eats his toes, then his ankles and the bones. Slowly, over hours I will lower him. When there are no nerves left to feel pain, when the acid is just below his heart, I will let the end of the chain drop that scum into hell."

# 11

*News Brazil—All Media*

*Silvina Arancha*

*July 4, 2013*

*Manaus*

*The Brazilian Spring*

*It was sparked by the increased cost of bus fare in Sao Paulo. The powder keg beneath the fuse is the spiraling cost of spending on the 2014 World Cup and 2016 Olympics. Over one million "beautiful people" took to the streets of all major cities in protest of wrongheaded priorities by their elected leaders.*

*The catalyst driving the citizenry to the barricades is the seeming utter disregard in resolving dire social issues. Over-the-top spending on the venues associated with these two events has sidelined needed public housing, transportation and education projects that were promised but are now on the backburner.*

*Brazil has long had a reputation for public works project corruption and shoddy work on those projects. That reputation is well earned and playing itself out as charges are flying over significant delays on*

*the public works projects and an overemphasis on World
Cup/Olympic venues.*

*The turnabout from the joy of four years ago when Brazil won the
right to host these sporting events is happening as costs are
skyrocketing for every, EVERY, element of World Cup and Olympic
work.*

*Multiple reports have surfaced of special benefits conceded to
Brazilian politicians.*

*In Manaus, the Amazon city hosting some of the events, over one
hundred thousand people demonstrated for the needed public works
improvements. Brazil is building an enormous fifty-two thousand
seat stadium for some of the World Cup and Olympic soccer
matches in Manaus. The stadium is expected to sit largely idle after
the Olympic Games since only 350 people on average regularly
attended soccer matches in the old thirty thousand seat stadium.
That average for attendance for a level four soccer team is the lowest
of any in Brazil.*

*The Sao Paulo bus fare increase put the ruling class and politicians
in the spotlight, and the protests around the country are demanding
they be held accountable. Nice, but expect more bus fare increases in
the future.*

**********

Sheets of rain blew across the street. The streets were flooded. The
aged sewer system was choking to death, drowning. It had been
raining for days in Manaus.

The chief engineer charged with building the Manaus Olymipic
Stadium shook his head. Another day lost for pouring cement. The
pressure of the timetable for completion was aggravating his high
blood pressure.

"No more chorizo, for you, Franco," Franco Ozat said to
himself as he burped. "Heartburn."

He had taken the managers responsible for various parts of the
project out the night before since heavy rain had been forecast. After

all, Chunk DeLuna was in town and wanted to meet with the men building his behemoth in the jungle.

"Fifty-two thousand seats! One of the largest stadiums in all of South America," DeLuna was saying at the long rectangular table seating the eleven men. "Here's to you!" and he raised his glass of beer.

The engineer feeling confident in his relationship with the owner of his company, stood. "Here's to you Mr. DeLuna. Thank you for your employment, and thank you for making us all proud of Brazil and this stadium."

The men all cheered, smiling. DeLuna stood, laughed and lifted his glass.

"Here's to the rain that allowed us to get together tonight and get a little drunk," Ozat said wobbling a bit as he slurred his words.

Carlos, always quiet but always at DeLuna's right hand, was glad to see DeLuna relaxing. Lately Chunk had been crazy. Well, crazier than usual. DeLuna was worried about everything. He began micromanaging every aspect of the business. Areas he had not been into in years he was poking his nose into. Even Lupe had a few more bruises than normal.

Chunk was a man under pressure. The process of securing contracts to build the stadium had been nothing more than the usual graft, bribery, arm twisting, and kidnapping. But the building, the actual building of a fifty-two thousand seat Olympic Stadium under a tight deadline with a very disciplined project management and oversight process was driving DeLuna to despair.

Yet, these were Carlos' responsibilities. He was president of CDL Enterprisa. It was Carlos who met multiple times a week with project managers or the Olympic project managers in Rio. It was Carlos who was guiding the project forward—on time if not on budget.

Maybe this really does mean something to DeLuna, Carlos rationalized. Maybe DeLuna seeks the recognition this will bring him and the company for successfully building the Manaus Stadium. Maybe Chunk is tired of the murders, the drugs and the whores. This was always the plan—to build a legitimate business and exit the criminal part of the enterprise. No more broke gamblers begging for more time or more credit. No more bruises for Lupe.

If DeLuna was not tired of seeing the battering Lupe took at his hands, Carlos was. But he knew Lupe could take it. She was tough. She was tougher than anyone in the gang, except Angel Pagan. Carlos knew she was tougher than him. He had seen her repeatedly stand up to DeLuna, to physically fight him, and he watched her get struck down every time. In front of him, Raphael, Pedro and Paco. And none of them did a thing to help Lupe. None of them stood up to DeLuna. Not much had changed from that day on the bridge so many years ago when Chunk struck them down in seconds and became leader of the Rei de Praia, the beach kings.

Something had to change. All of it was getting to DeLuna. The volcano, always boiling, was on the verge of eruption.

All of it was getting to Carlos—not the business. The business was easy. But the treatment of Lupe by DeLuna was wearing Carlos down. A man, a real man, does not treat a woman the way Chunk treats Lupe. Something stuck in Carlos' mind—Chunk never hit Lupe in front of Angel Pagan; he never even yelled at her in front of him. What did that mean? Pagan was the most brutal killer. He showed no mercy towards men or women. He had no compunction about torturing a woman; yet, it perplexed Carlos that Chunk was much more respectful to Lupe when Pagan was around.

# 12

*News Brazil—All Media*

*Silvina Arancha*

*July 26, 2013*

*Manaus*

*Is El Nino playing tricks on Brazil?*

*Along the northeast coast of Brazil, Jose Flores has been sweltering for several months now in his coco-frio stand on Boa Viagem beach, but west of here, almost two thousand miles west of here, deep in Amazonia, the city of Manaus is seeing record rains, day after day, week after week.*

*For denizens of the jungle, especially those living along the Amazon River and its tributaries, water has been rising to levels never seen before. In normal rainy seasons, water will rise along the rivers by twenty-thirty feet. This year many of the floating homes, ingenious devices to deal with the high water, have been tested with water rising forty to fifty feet. It is estimated that over thirty thousand homes floated away from the stanchions that held the rafts supporting them, creating a significant homeless problem deep in the interior.*

85

*Atmospheric scientists say this occurrence is a hundred-year phenomenon for Brazil. Winds that sweep in off the Atlantic, across northern Brazil out to the Andes, and then south to Argentina, are forming a blocking pattern that keeps heat in the east and rain in Amazonia. This year's El Nino seems to be adding its own kick to this witches' brew, but as Jose Flores says from his stand along this beautiful stretch of beach, "Who am I to complain. It's hot, but business is great. Hot weather, coco-frios sell like crazy."*

**********

For two hundred million years, flora and fauna piled high at the end of summer building a roof of decaying vegetation over the underground river. Above the earth's mantle and below the earthen rooftop, a great cavern existed. The cavern, nineteen miles long and one mile wide, gently guided the river through. As the rainy season peaked in the jungle, the river that carved the underground chasm began rising. This year the underground river would rise higher than it had in a thousand years and was scraping the limestone dome. Weighed down with hundreds of thousands of tons of concrete and steel for the Olympic stadium in Manaus, the dome began to sag.

*********

Taking their final line-of-sight measurements from the top of the stadium on fixed points on the horizon, the surveyor and his apprentice were alarmed at the variance.

"This measurement, you tool," the surveyor shouted at his apprentice, "it's wrong."

"What do you mean?"

"Look, these coordinates would show the stadium is a meter below the recording taken two years ago," the surveyor said.

Both men looked at the previously documented readings that were certified by the original engineering company.

"These readings today are mine, and they are not wrong," the apprentice began. "They are not wrong; look at the transit level yourself. You verify." The surveyor and his apprentice moved to all six key points on the property. The surveyor leveled his instrument to the horizon with the apprentice holding the rod in the distance. Once all six readings were completed, he stood back and looked at his apprentice.

"This can't be right."

"It is right. I know our instruments. They are perfectly calibrated. What it means is the original engineering company certified incorrect readings by the surveyor who did this work before us."

"Not possible. I know the engineer who certified it, and I went over them with him when I first came on board."

"Then how do we explain it?" asked the apprentice.

"I don't, unless the stadium is sinking," and the surveyor laughed.

With a still serious look about him, the apprentice replied, "That's not possible," and now with a slight smile, he asked, "Is it?" The two men looked at each other and began laughing loudly.

After their laugh the surveyor told the apprentice he would bring this to the attention of the project engineer.

*********

### August 5, 2013

9 a.m.—Angus Watt, project director, on the Manaus Olympic Stadium listened to what Franco Ozat, his chief engineer, had to say as Phase 2 of the Manaus stadium was ready to launch.

"Everything we've done to date looks good. We're ready to begin pouring the cement for the walls," Ozat report to his boss.

"What about that survey?" Watt asked, the deep wrinkles, in the brow of a man who is used to worrying, getting deeper. "There was a point last week when we closed Phase 1 where you said the surveyor was concerned that the final Phase 1 readings were off."

"Yes, he does not have an answer why the readings are showing up one meter lower than when we began," Ozat said.

"Do you think it's a mistake in what he recorded or do you think we're on a sinking ship," Watt laughed nervously.

"That's funny, boss," Ozat replied. "No, I think he made a mistake in the final reading. We're going to measure all six points again tomorrow morning."

"And you'll let the project go ahead and pour this afternoon?" a now angry Watt growled.

"No," he answered sheepishly.

"Damn right, no. Do the readings now," Watt commanded.

"Yes, sir."

*********

4 p.m.—"Confirmed," Ozat said as he stood in the doorway of Watt's office. "The surveyor made the error and has corrected it. The transit he was using was not calibrated and gave him a wrong reading."

"Good," Watt smiled. "For a while there, I pictured us descending into hell," he laughed.

"We may still get there, but it won't be because of the readings."

"We'll begin the pour first thing in the morning and fire that surveyor."

"I already did," Ozat said.

*********

Not shared with Watt were the conversations that Ozat participated in during the late morning and early afternoon.

11 a.m.—Franco Ozat brought Joao Silva in and after twenty minutes of arguing, the surveyor said, "The readings are correct, period. I always double-check the readings, and if anything is off, I go through the whole process of recalibrating the transit. I did two complete readings of all six points. My apprentice found the same variances. Four of the points are off—by a lot."

"How much off?" Ozat asked.

"All by one meter," Silva said.

"Then how do you explain this.?"

"I can't."

"Well if you can't, who can," Ozat pressed.

"I don't know, Franco. I really don't. I've never seen anything like this before," Silva said, genuinely puzzled.

"Let's make this easy. There are only two explanations, right?"

"Yes."

"Tell me them."

"Either the ground is sinking, or I'm totally wrong on all the points," Silva said matter-of-factly.

"Do you think the ground is sinking?" Ozat asked, somewhat cynically.

"No, I mean I don't think it is, but it has to be."

"Why?"

"Because I've been surveying for fifteen years. I know my craft," Silva said firmly. "I know my tools, and I know that the readings I took are absolutely accurate."

"Take your lunch break now and come back in two hours," Ozat told the frustrated surveyor.

*********

Noon—Ozat went to Carlos, the president of CDL, who was in Manaus for a review of the project and the man responsible for getting him the position of chief engineer on the stadium project.

"Something is very wrong, Carlos. We know from the independent survey of the land by the French geologists that there was the potential for underground water. But something more serious is occurring."

In Carlos' on-site office this day was Chunk DeLuna. DeLuna had come out for a visit; something he was doing more often as the overall Manaus project moved along. DeLuna said nothing as Carlos and the engineer, Ozat, discussed the problem.

"Tell me what our problems are. Prioritize them based on the information we have available," Carlos said in his direct way of identifying problems and then deciding how to solve them.

"First," Ozat began, "I do trust the surveyor. He is totally competent. What he is saying about the readings is true. Number two, the ground is sinking. I can't yet say if it's from the weight of what we've already put on the land, the foundation, the heavy equipment, or something natural, like the heavy spring rains we have had this year. The initial survey of the land said there was underground water. We assumed at the time that there might be runoff from a River Negro tributary. It now appears that is correct, but something bigger is occurring down there. Number three, what is underneath the stadium is larger than underground run off from the River Negro. It might be a large run-off or," Ozat paused, "I've heard of underground lakes, rivers.

"What are you talking about," DeLuna interrupted, "an underground lake? Have you been drinking?"

"No, Mr. DeLuna. It's just that something is causing the ground to sink." Ozat was a man in the middle; he was deeply indebted to DeLuna.

Ozat had frequently visited brothels the gang maintained in Manaus. In a drunken rampage, he accused a prostitute of stealing from his wallet, which she had. He punched her several times, which was recorded on the brothels camera system. Later the girl went missing, and when DeLuna called Ozat in, explained what he had been told by others at the brothel, it was assumed that somehow Ozat had murdered the girl and disposed of her. He was shown the film of himself hitting the girl viscously, her bleeding. "And you're telling me, Mr. Ozat, you do not know what happened to this girl. We have not seen her since this recording. What do you remember?" And Ozat remembered nothing. DeLuna's men had taken him to a hotel, smeared some of the girl's blood in the room, which Ozat saw when he awoke. Ozat at the time was convinced somehow he had beaten the girl at the brothel, taken her to a hotel and possibly killed her, later disposing of the body. DeLuna said he needed to report the girl missing to the police and share what he knew with them. When Ozat begged, cried and offered DeLuna anything he wanted, DeLuna relented and promised to help the man. Unsaid was that DeLuna had simply moved the girl to another of his brothels, in Salvador, where she recovered from a few bruises.

As DeLuna was saying, "What are you talking about, an underground lake. Have you been drinking?" that horrible night came rushing back to Ozat's mind.

DeLuna continued. "Well, I'll tell you what it isn't, it isn't a lake. And it isn't a river. This project is going forward without any dumb excuses. You get rid of that surveyor and fix those readings."

"Chunk, a word," Carlos said, and nodded to the engineer to stay seated.

"Stop," DeLuna said to Carlos, stubbornly, "No word. You," he said pointing to Ozat, "fix the survey so it satisfies whatever is needed and no more talk about underground rivers."

The engineer said, "Yes, sir."

Carlos nodded.

The engineer left the two.

"Good, I'm off. Heading back to Lupe tonight."

"Chunk ..."

"Carlos, I know. But what the hell are we supposed to do. The walls are going up tomorrow. You tell that project manager he's got an underground river, the whole thing stops. They stop—we lose millions in missed deadline penalties."

"What if it is sinking?"

"Carlos, it is sinking. Didn't you listen to Franco? We can't do anything about it. The ground sinks a little bit. This isn't quicksand here. The stadium will stay up. Stop worrying."

# PART

3

# 13

Lupe Monserrat was part of the physical melting pot of Brazil. Her father's parents were a mix of African and Portuguese, and her mother's heritage was Dutch/Portuguese and Kayapo Indian, natives of Amazonia. It was the Kayapo that Lupe most associated with. As a girl growing up, her mother and grandmother shared stories, passed down in the native Brazilian oral tradition, of her great grandfather who was chief of all the Kayapo. "All" the Kayapo consisted of rain forest tribes amounting to around four thousand natives living in a series of villages along the great Amazon watershed more than a thousand miles inland, directly west of Recife.

It was this chief, Punatira, who stood up to invasion of the rain forest in the 1800s. He held road building at bay. He was revered for his persistence in protecting his lands from invasion. In the end it was ironic that he died from measles, contracted from the human invaders. By the 1970s the tribe had neared extinction and was estimated at less than one thousand individuals when laws started being passed to protect the rain forest and its inhabitants living along the rivers. It was Lupe's great grandmother who took her grandmother and left the jungle with one of the "outsiders" and settled in Recife. Lupe's grandmother delighted in telling Lupe and her siblings tales from the rainforest.

As Lupe's awareness of the world grew, so did her dream of visiting the inland rain forest and her roots. "Chunk, it's important to me. I have always wanted to see where my grandmother came from, to see the rain forest," she told DeLuna.

"I like the idea; we will do it."

Surprised, since DeLuna rarely did anything spontaneously, Lupe said, "Yes, Chunk? Really? When?"

They had just finished breakfast on veranda of the oceanside villa; DeLuna stood up and said, "Soon. I have to go to Manaus in a couple of weeks."

"Oh, Chunk, that's wonderful."

"Talk with your mother and father, get everything put together and I'll get you there."

Lupe got up, and put her arms around DeLuna, "Sometimes you can be the dearest man in the world," and she kissed him on the lips, something very rare for Lupe. She and DeLuna existed together. There was no love, more mutual need satisfied.

Aroused, he put his hand on her rear and said, "Let's go upstairs."

"Later, I want to call my mother," and she pulled out of the embrace and started to move inside.

"OK, later. When you talk with her, see if she wants to come along, the three of us and the pilot."

"She's never been in a plane, but she'll want to go. I know it."

"We will take a small plane, most likely there will only be a small landing strip. Warn her it will be a long flight. It will take hours to get Manaus. I think where you said they came from is somewhere between here and Manaus. So a few days in the jungle and a couple of days in Manaus. You'll like Manaus.

"A vacation. I love it. Thank you, Chunk," and she pressed into him again, fully six inches taller than DeLuna, her breasts pushed into his face.

The bull swept her up in his arms, an awkward picture, her long body poking out legs and arms on either side of him. But the bull was strong, and he carried her easily inside the mansion.

\*\*\*\*\*\*\*\*

Ten days later their plane banked over Boa Viagem beach and turned westward. The four-passenger Cessna was over a blanket of green that stretched unbroken for over two thousand miles. The journey to the land of the Kayapo would cover thirteen hundred miles; in the turbo, it tested the limits of fuel to reach the small jungle airport.

In the week before they embarked on the journey, Lupe and her mother made contacts with the tribe though Amazon Adventures. This touring organization would provide them with a pilot who was a native speaker and would be their guide, arranging daily tours throughout their visits with the Kayapo along the Rio Xingu where Kayapo villages were clustered and later in Manaus. Thinking of the three days the guide would spend helping to introduce Lupe and her mother to distant relatives had Lupe in a high state of anxiety.

The plane dropped out of the clouds, and looking over the pilot's shoulder, Lupe was prepared to crash. Ahead and down were nothing but trees as far as she could see. Then a large river appeared off to the right. The plane followed it, and after several minutes Lupe could see the airfield. "Chunk, please tell me that is not where we are landing." Chunk did not need to answer for at that moment the pilot pointed the nose of the plane straight down. "Hold on lady; that's our airport." Lupe froze as they set down thirty seconds later.

Arriving at the dirt runway carved out of the canopy and near the tribe's village along the river, the visitors were not sure what to expect. The "airport" was the grass strip, a small building with a corrugated steel roof and a gas tank. Chunk asked the pilot how the tribe was able to get gas to the tank in this wilderness. He was told it came by boat; DeLuna found that somehow odd.

To their surprise, when the plane landed dozens of tribe members came to greet them as they exited the plane. Apparently the return of "daughters" of the tribe was a big deal, especially a great-granddaughter and a granddaughter of the esteemed chief Punatira.

Members of the tribe were adorned in colorful headdresses made from bird feathers, body paint, arm bands, and not much else. For the next three days they talked through the guide with their distant relatives. They took canoe trips up river fishing. They swam nearly naked every morning and late in the afternoon in the river. Chunk was surprised at the resemblance Lupe and her mother had to the women of the tribe, the facial bone structure. The exception was that Lupe was a giant among the people of the tribe.

"Are you sure you are not from here, boss?" the pilot asked DeLuna.

"Really, Chunk," Lupe remarked. "You are the same size as everyone here."

"Except for this," Chunk said, holding his right arm up and flexing a powerful bicep.

Members of the tribe who had been sitting on the bank of the river saw the huge muscle, and two boys who had become friendly with DeLuna came over to touch it.

"Maybe I should have them touch this," DeLuna said to Lupe pointing to his crotch.

"You pig, do not dare to do that."

On the second day, the Kayapo guide arranged a river tour. Lupe's mother opted to stay in the village and communicate with some of the women she had made fast friends with using her small knowledge of Kayapo language.

"Normally, we can't go up river on some of these smaller streams," the guide was telling Lupe and Chunk, "but with the rain that's been coming down all season, the streams themselves have become rivers. You will see sights no one but natives have ever seen," he said as they boarded a long, flat-bottomed boat the size of two canoes and with a decent sized motor purring in the back. Chunk and Lupe sat midboat, he in back of her. The tour guide sat up front facing them, and a native Kayapo was the boat's helmsman.

Fog was rising off the river as the early morning rain gave way to the rising sun; the humidity was rising faster. Heading northwest on the Xingu River, they came upon a swollen tributary, and the guide nodded to the helmsman. Immediately, the landscape changed as they entered the tributary. On a bare branch of a drowned tree, that hung just above their heads, sat two large parrots, one a red head and the other a blonde. The birds watched as the boat passed beneath them, their long colorful tail feathers inches above Lupe's head. She turned to continue watching them. "They are beautiful," she said to no one.

The ever polite tour guide said, "Yes, miss."

Now the tributary entry to this hidden land widened from ten feet to forty feet. It widened again a short time later to fifty yards putting them fully in the sun as it rose further in the sky. Chunk watched as the boat was passing by a floating house on the right bank. The rising stream had lifted the structure not built on stilts but on a raft. If the river rose, the home rose. On the edge of the house's raft, that also served as a front porch, a young girl who was pretty but fat sat with her legs dangling in the river. A small brown monkey with a bald head sat on her lap. Noticing the boat, the monkey began screeching. The fat girl stroked the creature's head, and it calmed down. Lupe exchanged smiles with the girl.

Further upstream a plant, with man-sized leaves, listed over the water. "Lupe stand up. I want to get a picture of you with one of those leaves in the background," he said raising his iPhone. Lupe stood as the helmsman, not understanding Portuguese but picking up on the movement of Lupe, slowed the boat, putting it into reverse. As the phone's camera snapped the backdrop of the 7-foot-high, heart shaped leaf it began surrounding Lupe, wrapping its edges around her as the boat came to a stop. The helmsman stood, grabbed a machete from under his seat, reached to the right of Lupe and hacked at the stem, causing the leaf to fall away from her into the water.

"What was that?" Lupe asked, stunned for a moment, more aware of the helmsman advancing towards her with a machete than the leaf, which she only felt at the same second the helmsman cut it down.

The guide spoke to the helmsman in Kayapo. "He says it is a naughty tree." They continued talking, and the guide said, "He says it is very unusual; most Gunnera leaves calm. He only saw one move like this one other time. He says that one hung over water also. But he says it would not hurt the lady, it just liked her."

"Lupe, I kept snapping, I couldn't believe what was happening. Look, it's part way around you."

"That's creepy, but I love it. Do not delete that picture. We will have fun with it at home. I want to blow it up and frame it. A picture of it, as big as it is."

"Nice," was all the enthusiasm Chunk could muster.

After a time, their boat reentered the River Xingu upstream. The Amazon Adventures guide arranged for a late lunch at one of the floating homes that doubled as a restaurant for tourists to the area. The menu almost made Lupe pass out with a combination of eel, ants and snake. Chunk tried the wild boar, while Lupe settled for a plate of fruit with guava and mango.

In the afternoon they went further up river. The helmsman shut the engine off, ruddered the boat around, and it began to slowly float downstream. "Your senses will sharpen now," the guide offered.

Chunk did not know what he meant, but Lupe heard it right away—silent but noisy. No longer the man-made grind of the twenty horsepower engine; now nature's noise as millions of creatures went about living their lives: pops, cackles, hisses, splashes, chopping, poking, munching, and wind. Directly in front of them, Chunk saw a bird flitting along low picking up bugs from the surface of the river. Then, snatch! It was gone.

"Did you see that?" he said to Lupe.

"Yes. Where did that bird go? What was that?"

The guide turned around to see what they were talking about but did not see anything.

The helmsman turned the rudder so the boat was now heading directly for where the bird disappeared. "Arapaima," he said.

"What?" Lupe said. "Something came up out of the water and ate that bird."

"Arapaima," the helmsman said again and pointed to the left. "Look," the guide said as a great grey object surfaced, coughed, and slowly glided past the boat. It was half as long as the boat and headed up river.

Chunk pulled his iPhone out and caught the full length of the 9-foot-long fish on camera. Chunk and Lupe, peering intently at the path of the fish, looked up at the helmsman.

"Arapaima," he confirmed.

They both laughed as did the guide and helmsman at seeing one of the unique beasts of the Amazon watershed. The guide and helmsman talked in Kayapo for a moment.

"He said the arapaima has a snout longer and wider than an anteater. He calls the fish the Amazon of the Amazon. Quite harmless, but very, very big."

"Very, very big," Chunk agreed.

"And scary," Lupe added. "At least when you first see it. Can you ask him why it comes out of the water like that?"

More conversation took place between the front of the boat and the back of the boat.

"He says it comes up for air. It breathes, that's what that cough was, him gasping for air. Plus, he apparently eats small birds."

"Weird," Chunk said. Still, he was glad he had a picture to show his boys back at CDL Enterprisa. And just as quickly he put the thought of CDL out of his mind. He was peaceful here and wanted to stay that way.

Lupe looked over the side of the boat to see if she could see another arapaima. The water was barely moving. She smiled at her reflection, then she saw a sinewy object on the surface snaking its way toward the boat. It was large and very long.

"Back," the helmsman commanded taking a long pipe to his mouth and spitting a poison dart to the snake's head, killing the green anaconda.

Lupe looked at Chunk. She was shaking. Chunk looked at the guide who was speaking to the helmsman.

"Strange day, he said. He's never seen an arapaima and an anaconda on the same day. They are both rare."

"And big. This must be our lucky day," DeLuna said laughing. "If we survive." The guide translated and the four travelers in the boat laughed, Lupe nervously.

Lupe inhaled. She could smell the jungle, the mustiness, the green and the oxygen being created. After a time, she looked cautiously into the river again. It was so clear she felt she could drink it. She could see small fish swimming by; towards the bank she saw long blades of grass flowing beneath the surface. Reflections of vultures circling above were on the surface of the water.

The boat seemed not to move as it was carried along by the flowing Xinga. Chunk was laying back; his hands behind his head watching the clouds above. Lupe sat in solitude: her back straight, her hands folded in her lap, her head turned slightly to the right as if listening. She felt a pocket of cool air cross her forehead, face and chest. The cooler air had come from above and just as quickly she was re-enveloped in jungle steam. Her eyes darted from object to object along the shore: a large purple orchid beneath a leafy palm tree; yellow melon-like fruit of the passion flower vine hung above a pink Flamingo poking along in shallow water; a clutch of green parrots, maybe fifty of them, all exactly the same size were making a racket. Long red-tinted, finger-like leaves hung from branches on the opposite shore. Butterflies flapped about crazily around purple cone-shaped flowers dropping out of a mass of vines hanging from treetops. The gray of Recife came to Lupe's mind and then faded as the picture of this world of color with a great green frame around it excited her eyes.

The boat bent around the entrance to the stream, and they were nearing the village, Chunk reached in vain from his reclining position; he was trying to plunk a banana from a tree leaning over the smaller waterway. The boat slid up to the dock and tie-up. The helmsman took a boomerang and flung it side arm at a papaya tree. The tool sliced into the stem dropping a cluster of the succulent green fruit to the ground. As they got off the boat, he handed each of them one of the papayas. The four sat on the dock, legs dangling into the water, and they talked about their day and ate the papayas. Lupe kept her eye out for anything slithering on the water, snapping her legs up and out as a fish surfaced to get a bug.

On their third day visiting with the Kayapo, Chunk went fishing in the morning, a long walk through tall grass to a favorite village fishing spot. Lupe and her mother stayed with the guide and women from the tribe. They listened to stories of the tribe's history. Lupe shared stories of life in the city of Recife. The native Kayapo and the Recifians were each amazed at other's way of life.

On the grass by the river bank in the late afternoon, the sun was oppressive, but the river brought a cool breeze. Fourteen people from the tribe and their four guests relaxed in the power plant of the earth. The guide related stories from the tribe, and the Kayapo helmsman communicated information shared by Lupe and her mother. Chunk sat next to Lupe, put his arm around her and pulled her back on the grass. They lay there, looking up, listening to screeching birds further off in the jungle, and the patter of the Kayapo's speech, of their eagerness to talk about their culture. Lupe thought, "This is good." DeLuna glanced to his left looking at a naked woman, except for a loin cloth and thought, "This is good."

DeLuna said to Lupe, "I could live here."

"No way you could live here," she laughed.

"I could, me among the beasts. King of the jungle!"

The two of them laughed. DeLuna had no fear, not of the jaguars the villagers feared, not of snakes, which they had come in contact several times, nor of getting lost. He was at home. As he floated off into a light sleep in the comfort of new friends, he wondered why civilization was so angry and combative and here in the wild it was so peaceful. The beast was tamed.

On the morning of the fourth day, as they were leaving, many members of the tribe came to say good-bye to their "family." They walked together, in rows of five or six in a long parade-like column. Lupe, her mother and the chief led the way; DeLuna hung back with the pilot and the guide, letting Lupe and her mother enjoy this moment in the sun. The chief, dressed in a bright ceremonial robe, colorful face paint and a headdress, held an enormous parrot on his arm. The bird was a rainbow of feathers.

Lupe had seen the magnificent parrot two days earlier. As she passed by the chief's large river house that rested on a raft, she heard the bird speak, like it knew her. The chief had trained the bird well—a stray dog walked past and the bird barked at it. Lupe laughed so hard she cried. The bark was so real the dog was startled and ran off. Even the humorless DeLuna cracked a smile. "Chunk," Lupe began, "I need that bird."

Standing beside the guide and interpreter the chief said, "Thank you for coming home. To help you always remember your family we have a present for you. I give you Puckerlips; I understand you found him very amusing." He stretched out his arm to Lupe, and as she heard his words and the gift they conveyed, she put out her arm. Lupe flashed a knowing glance at Chunk. A tribe member quickly put a burlap cloth on Lupe's arm as the bird hopped from the Chief's forearm to Lupe's. She pulled back at first as the claws clamped on and through the burlap. She winced, but Lupe kept her arm up. She knew it was an honor. A bird. Her bird. Puckerlips.

# 14

Through her years with Chunk DeLuna, Lupe Monserrat had changed. While Chunk had grown richer and more powerful, Lupe grew in knowledge; she became stronger. After her trip to Amazonia, she became more curious. She read, became widely read, not only of all the great South American writers like Coelho, Amado, Allende, Llosha, and Neruda, particularly Neruda, the love poet of Chile, but also the French, Russians and Spanish. Since DeLuna would not allow children in their relationship, Lupe had pets—the parrot, Puckerlips, and DeLuna's dog, Cortito, who by then was ancient in dog years.

Lupe's days were spent doing simple things. She lived a life other women envied, particularly those who lived four streets back from the beach in the public housing projects where Lupe had her beginnings. She played games: paddle ball on the beach, tennis at the beach club and volleyball with a women's league. She yearned for more speed in her life. Not a fast life like Chunk led, that was dangerous. But she wanted more; she was restless.

Lupe had several miscarriages, really forced abortions. Chunk was not ready to be a parent; he would never be ready to be a parent. Lupe was. She wanted a child, children.

So with time on her hands, Lupe continued to search. A greenhouse was added to the rear of the Mediterranean villa; she became a plant lady for a while. She tended exotic stalks with giant leaves from deep in the Amazon; she watered tiny, delicate ferns from the Andes. She watered the flaming red torch ginger and placed several Amazon sword plants floating on top of a large round disk in the entry foyer. Late in the mornings, she would have green tea on the patio between the greenhouse and the ocean.

One day as Adonis, her houseman, served her breakfast, she said to him while breathing deeply, "this is so lovely I could eat it."

"Yes, Miss, your breakfast?"

"No, Adonis, I mean the air. It is so fresh and clean," Lupe smiled and took in the sea breeze.

"Yes, Miss. The air is beautiful this morning.

"And the sky," she continued, "is so clear today. It is like it was just born. I should get my camera and capture its beauty."

"You should paint it, Miss," Adonis replied.

"Paint it," Lupe replied, "You're funny, Adonis. I can't paint."

"You are an artist, Miss. Everything you do, you do with beauty."

"Obrigada, Adonis," she thanked him. "But how would anyone be able to paint this," and she stood, casting her arms out wide.

"My friend, Estephan, he can paint this," Adonis said proudly, "Estephan could teach you to paint this."

"Painting is so slow; I'd go crazy," Lupe smiled, bringing her arms down and sitting as if exhausted from thinking about it.

"Estephan says people are in too much of a hurry. Their lives will be over, and they will never have lived them."

Lupe looked at Adonis. The thought he expressed struck her. "What else does your friend say?"

"He is wise among my neighbors. He says painting helps you have greater insights. By taking time to focus on one portion of life, closely, for days, you get to admire God's genius," Adonis said looking off towards the ocean, smiling, and thinking of his friend.

Lupe smiled also. She thought, if I never take up painting, I would still like to meet a man who thinks like that.

*********

The next day, as she finished her afternoon swim, Adonis brought Lupe a towel. "Adonis, does your friend the painter have a studio. I would like to see his paintings."

"He does, Miss."

"Then tomorrow afternoon, instead of swimming, I would like you to take me there."

"Yes, Miss," Adonis said, happy that Lupe would trust his judgment about this friend.

**********

The following afternoon, at 2 p.m., Adonis pulled the Audi A8 around to the front of the house, and Lupe got in the front passenger seat.

"Wouldn't you be more comfortable in the rear seat, Miss?" Adonis said, mindful of his position.

"Yes, I would normally, but today I go with you as a friend to meet your friend."

Adonis felt like life had just changed. He knew it had not, but for a moment he was no longer beneath anyone—just one moment.

"Where is your friend's studio, Adonis?" Lupe asked looking at her driver.

"In the old part of Recife, on the south side, by the river."

"Well then, off we go, my friend," Lupe exclaimed, excited, a new venture ready to unfold. She hoped.

**********

The studio of Adonis' friend, the painter, was in an old mill building on the Capibaribe River in south Recife. The artist's studio was on the second floor that had a long corridor and no other tenants.

Adonis held the door for Lupe as they entered, and she was immediately struck by a large wide mural on the wall to her right. The studio itself was an open rectangle that had four large square windows in the center overlooking the river and the deep green treetops beyond. To the left there were partitioned areas, where in one, an older man was talking with three women and a young man.

106

Lupe assumed the older man was Adonis' friend since he was the only one talking and the only one without a brush and easel.

"I told Estephan we would be by about this time," Adonis said to Lupe, who was ever aware that every arranged time in Brazil was "on or about." There was just no need to hurry. "He said he would be finishing up about this time," and he gestured towards the seats on the right, "Why don't we sit."

"You sit; I'm just going to look around."

Lupe drifted from one painting to another on the walls to the left and the partitioned area. There were many styles, some good, some awful. There were two or three particularly stunning paintings, centered in the midst of the good and awful. Lupe assumed those were the instructor's.

Someone began playing a guitar from one of the portioned areas out of Lupe's sight. Then she heard humming, even soft singing accompanying the guitar. Lupe walked back to the center of the large open area and could see the old instructor sitting on a stool playing the guitar and his students finalizing strokes or beginning to clean brushes. The three women and the young man were swinging their hips. Lupe thought the attractive young man was doing the best job of hip movement. She thought someone should be painting that.

After several minutes passed and his students were leaving, the instructor walked to where Lupe was standing looking at the large mural.

"I am Estephan," he said extending his hand to Lupe.

"I am Lupe. Adonis had told me about you; thank you for letting us come by," Lupe said glancing toward Adonis who remained seated and who now waved to Estephan.

"My good friend. It was kind of him to bring you here. He says you are an artist," Estephan said.

"No, no." Lupe denied, snapping a glance to Adonis. "Why would he say that?"

"Oh, forgive me. He did not say you painted. It was the way he described what you do, how you do things that led me to conclude you were an artist," Estephan said smiling, revealing teeth that while no longer white, and had become beige with age, were nonetheless strong, well aligned and with a gold front tooth made his smile a bit enchanting.

"I will have a talk with my friend," Lupe said with a wry smile, that was appreciative of Adonis' awareness.

"Go easy on him; he is always very respectful when he speaks of you."

"OK," she said glancing at Adonis. Then turning back to the instructor, "Tell me about this mural. It is captivating."

"It is the jungle, Amazonia, our country," he said proudly and began pointing to different trees and birds hidden among them.

"Is that a panther?" Lupe asked. She realized that in among the jungle and the many shades of green and brown the artist had cleverly concealed the animals, birds and even insects of the jungle.

"You have good eyes," said Estephan, looking at Lupe's eyes.

"And here ... that bird," she said, continuing to unravel the embedded secrets.

"Yes."

"And a snake," she gasped, realizing there was a large green and black snake curling down from an upper branch of the painting. It was almost invisible in its camouflage.

"You are seeing my jungle. Very good, very quick."

Stepping back several feet Lupe took in the entire painting that was about thirty-five feet wide and ten feet high. "You did this, all of this?"

"Yes," he said, and cast his eyes down.

Lupe was struck. Such an enormous, intricate work. Why did he appear so humble about it. She pointed to other paintings on the walls and on the partitions opposite the mural. "And these, are more of your paintings among them?" And immediately catching herself she said, "Let me see if I can find them!" she exclaimed, excited about the game she was creating.

Estephan Kelly assented with a nod and smiled.

Lupe walked to the wall on the left of the entryway and pointed to a landscape in the middle. Estephan nodded. On one of the partitions, to the left, she pointed to a portrait. Estephan nodded again. Then on the far right of the partitioned areas by the leftmost large square window, she identified a still life. He smiled.

"Pretty good, huh?" she said, pleased with herself. "I got all of yours, right?"

"No. You missed two."

Lupe was red faced, "Let me look again." And she proceeded to walk among the seventy or so paintings that hung on the studio walls. Stumped, she felt she could not identify any others without insulting the instructor; they were all so awful.

"Do you need help?" he toyed with her.

"Yes," she said as Estephan walked to first one terrible painting of a cow and a second terrible painting of the sea. "These two are also mine."

Her red face got redder.

"Let me help you. I'll give you the first answer, and you give me the second," he said, playing a game that Lupe did not understand but nodded she would play.

"All of the paintings on this wall are from students, beginning painters, except the three you correctly identified. I put many of my students' first paintings, including mine, on the wall for them to be proud of those early works, even if they stink," Estephan, the instructor, said.

Lupe laughed out loud, and put her hand over her mouth.

He continued, "Yes, quite bad, right?"

She laughed again and decided to rib him, "Especially your two."

They both laughed; he placed a hand on her shoulder as he doubled over. "Now," he said, "are you ready for the second part?"

"Yes," she said with a smile, warming to his sense of play.

"OK, why are my other three paintings here among all this stuff," he laughed.

Lupe looked at the three paintings she had correctly identified. The landscape, the portrait and the still life. She stared at them. Why these three, she thought, they were all so different.

"They're different. That's why they're there," she jumped. "That's it isn't it," she squealed like a teenager, knowing she was right.

The gold tooth was gleaming as he smiled. "Yes," and before he could go on she jumped in place. "Whoa," he said. "But why are they different?"

"Whoops," she audibled. She put her thinking cap back on again. The landscape was outside; the other two could be done inside. The landscape was of nature—trees on a hillside that rolled down to the ocean. The portrait was of a person sitting—a man posed sideways with a large pointed nose and wavy black hair. The still life was of a vase of flowers—many types, many colors. Then she said these things represented different styles and the different subjects. All the while Estephan listened intently as the young woman spoke.

"My friend, Adonis, was right. Lupe, you are an artist. You should paint," Estephan said, and added, "Will I have the pleasure of hanging one of your awful first paintings on my wall?"

Lupe laughed as did Estephan. She looked at him. "Maybe," she said coyly. Tickled, she felt like she was being propositioned by this older but charming man. "Maybe."

# 15

Lupe Monserrat had become vivacious, breath-catchingly attractive in how she presented herself. Her hair was big, curly, and fell off to the right side. She had an oval face; her chin formed a V emphasizing gleaming white teeth when she smiled, which was increasingly less often. She dressed in clothes that allowed a lot of skin to show. She was fit, taut and well-tanned. Her clothes were always tight to emphasize the curves of her fitness and light colored to contrast her sun-darkened olive skin. Necklines on her blouses plunged to show off jewelry dropping between her small firm breasts; the straps of her sleeveless t-tops were thin and emphasized wonderfully toned arms. Wherever Lupe went, people, men and women, did a double take when they noticed her.

After moving in with Chunk years before, Lupe continued to grow in height and was now five feet nine inches tall to DeLuna's five foot three inches. Next to him she looked even taller. The difference was telling—she so well put together, tall and thin, he was short and wide. Lupe looked to be an athlete, and she was. In her pursuits of running, beach volleyball, dancing, and tennis she excelled. Only four months into tennis and she had the strongest serve of any woman at the Recife Beach Club.

For all the satisfaction she received from sports, a new interest, painting, was captivating her. She found she could lose herself in her painting, not think about the pain in her life.

Lupe did not think about Chunk while they were apart. It was important that she segment him off when they were not together; he was such a dominating, demanding presence when they were together. While the girl had grown straight and radiant, DeLuna had grown thicker, tougher and more threatening. A conflict brewed in Lupe. Chunk had rescued her from poverty, was good to her, fulfilling any wishes, but increasingly she felt poorer. She wanted more—not wealth, or things to buy—Lupe wanted love. Yes, she knew, Chunk loved her in his own barbaric way, and she did care about him. But now there was an ache inside her; something was missing. She wanted to care for a man, tenderly touch him, kiss his lips and hours later to still be able to feel that kiss. She knew she did not love Chunk, not romantically. They did not kiss, and when he did those things to her when making his form of love, she never felt relieved, never fulfilled, just exhausted. Lupe needed something more. Maybe painting would help. Lupe decided to take lessons from Adonis's friend.

Estephan Kelly, her instructor, was perhaps forty years older than Lupe. He looked even older, bent as he was from years of arching his back painting at his easels. She took classes with three other students, and she found his simple method of encouragement exhilarating. No one had ever inspired her to express a talent; yet here was this kindly man, older than her father, quietly speaking soft praise.

Weeks into her lessons, Lupe wanted to paint Puckerlips, the parrot she received as a gift on her visit to Amazonia. She loved Puckerlips' colors, his long feathers and extended tail. The big bird always had a gleam in its eye, like it was thinking of something to say. Lupe wanted to capture that.

Estephan allowed Lupe to bring the bird to class with the simple admonition after the first hour: "He can stay if he can keep his trap shut." Lupe had a signal for the bird to be quiet; she raised her right hand from left to right in front of him. As if to say, "Zip it." It worked.

As the painting of the bird began its second month, Estephan was beguiled by the beauty of Lupe's painting. Long strokes, overlaid with a light dabbing to capture the bird's grain, its texture; mixing colors carefully Lupe worked to bring out the real reds, blues and greens in his feathers. It was here that Estephan gave Lupe hints, almost whispers, but left it to her to create the bird on canvas. He could paint the bird, but he could see it was important that Lupe be the creator of this work.

One afternoon, late, when the others in the class had left and Estephan was cleaning brushes, Lupe came to him. She looked at the older man admiringly, then tenderly. She leaned toward the slightly built, taller man and kissed him on the lips. He pulled back sharply, a reaction to something not expected; a smile crossed his face, baring the one gold tooth in front. Lupe leaned forward again, placed her hands on either side of his head and kissed him again, full on his lips. He did not rear back. He put his hands on the edges of her shoulders and sank into her lips, moving his lips to the motion of Lupe's.

A distant memory evoked from his past, the soft lips of another girl, his wife. Long forgotten was the feeling he was now experiencing, of what he was now thankful for, for what was awakening in this kindly man.

The kiss lasted long, and after a time it ended. It had reached its end. Lupe did not pull back; Estephan did not pull back. The kiss simply ended. They looked at each other intently. Estephan moved to kiss Lupe again, aroused now. She pulled back slowly, put a finger tip to his lips.

Estephan was bewitched, but the fun was over. However, not in his head. He kept the thought of the younger woman in his mind. Fidelity is not the strong suit of many Brazilian artists who teach needy women. The temptations are always present with these eager students. But until this day, Estephan had never wavered. The opportunities had been fleeting in the past; but never had he felt so full so quickly ... well, not in so many years.

Lupe had never kissed a man that way with such a strong feeling of ... gratitude ... for how he made her feel. She found herself singing on the ride home. Where was this happiness coming from? Was this a mirror into herself, that she felt this good about herself she shared it with Estephan? Or did she really care for the man? She felt the later. After all, even though older he was handsome, still physically fit. She could feel the strength in his hands and arms as he held her shoulders, and when he did reach one arm around her back, she felt a shiver. That was when the kiss broke; it had excited her.

Now she felt bad about pulling back when Estephan came forward. She hoped he did not read the wrong message. Lupe was indeed eager, so eager she felt her pulse quicken at the thought; so eager she hoped she would have the courage to follow that kiss up with another.

Estephan was also singing on the way home. It was a song he used to listen to and sing years ago. He sang the words, "your kiss is on my lips," and visualized Lupe's kiss. He thought, "Estephan, you must paint that kiss. You must capture it, for you are never going to get another one." He laughed as he stepped off the bus near his home. A woman coming onto the bus avoided the laughing man with the gold tooth. As he walked along, he thought, "How do you paint a kiss?" He told himself he would.

# 16

The old Portuguese church of Sao Pedro was half full. The Tuesday mass was a high funeral for an undertaker in Olinda. At the rear of the church a few old ladies were scattered about like seeds in a field, not in neat rows. They were of a mind that attended mass every day, whether funeral, wedding or daily ritual. Amongst them was a lone young woman, her head respectfully covered with a veil. She was kneeling, deep in prayer. Unlike the slouching, butt-on-the-bench grandmothers, this younger woman was vertical, from head to knees; a perfect line of posture.

While the young woman was still, inside her turmoil raged as she debated, she believed, with God. "Yes, I can attain heaven by being myself," her mouth moved without sound.

The inner voice replied, "You cannot be doing what you are doing and still come to me."

"Look at me, not him. I don't do anything wrong."

"You are part of it," God said. "Part of him."

"I live; I do not kill."

"You have abortions," the spirit said.

"I DO NOT!" Lupe screamed inside, loud enough that sound escaped her lips. The old women in the pews turned their heads, looking in her direction. Lupe's lips tightened as she replied, "HE KILLS MY BABIES," and she lifted her head, looking towards the altar. "He kills others, not me."

"Who is it that enjoys the fruits of his sins, these murders he commits?" God asked her from the altar.

"I live with that man. I do love him, somehow. He did rescue me from that life. He treats me well. He cares for me," she pleaded.

"You cannot call aborting your children and beating you caring for you!" God spoke.

"I did not say it wasn't difficult; it is. I would rather not get beaten, but I am strong. I can take it. I told him I didn't want abortions. I want the babies. He has the problem; he doesn't want children. What am I going to do, leave him?" she asked herself.

"Yes," came God's answer from inside Lupe.

"How? My world is there. I only see him two or three nights a week and on weekends. He's gone otherwise," she persisted, seeking the right answer.

"He's gone doing his business, his evil. You are a part of this."

"I AM NOT," she shrieked at God.

Lupe was exhausted. She made the sign of the cross on her head, chest and shoulders and rose. It was Chunk's birthday; she needed to get him a cake.

*****************

"The Mexicans are idiots," Chunk was holding court on his patio by the pool. His gang was there with their women as Lupe arrived home.

"They behead people, put them up on posts after they kill them," he grinned. "You can kill your enemies but don't call attention to yourselves."

Carlos chimed in proudly, "Not one of us for the past six years has ever been arrested."

Chunk had invited two new members into his inner circle: a drug overlord from Rio named Chiba, and Jose Florinda, a pimp from Olinda who now managed three brothels for DeLuna in Manaus, the large city in the Amazon rain forest on the River Negro. DeLuna wanted to instill in them "his way" of doing business.

"When Carlos was younger," Chunk laughed, lifting his drink, "he did a lot of stupid things, robbing people in broad daylight, not

116

thinking through a hit, letting a witness live, etcetera, etcetera. But I taught him how to survive," DeLuna concluded as Carlos winced at being made an example. Carlos thought, you don't do that to the number two man in the organization. Then he thought, that was Chunk's way.

But Carlos supported his boss's bragging, "Yes he did, and we're free because of it."

Chunk continued, "Now, I'm not saying you got to be soft, not at all. You have to be quiet: no cops, no press, no problems."

"How do you keep out of the press," Florinda asked.

"What do you mean, Florinda from Olinda," Chunk laughed at the rhyme he made as he addressed the pimp.

"I mean when you kill people, when you cut off the head of your enemy, how do you keep it quiet?" Florinda questioned.

"Jesus Christ Almighty," Lupe exploded, not quite over her conversation with God. "You're talking about killing people like you're talking about a soccer game," she paused, standing by the pool. She put her hands on her hips, "Chunk, it's your birthday. Let's have fun."

Chunk looked at her. With his fifth drink in him, he was unsteady on his feet as he rushed at Lupe. He put his hands on her biceps, raised her up and launched her into the pool, fully clothed. When Lupe came to the surface, Chunk said, "You're right, Lupe. That was fun!" He laughed and looked at his compatriots who were in stitches at the spontaneity of DeLuna's action.

Only Carlos frowned. He had a soft spot for Lupe and did not like the way Chunk treated her. Lupe had taken many a beating that would have been delivered to him if not for her intervention. He felt she was too good for DeLuna. Carlos walked to the pool, reached his long arms down and clasping Lupe's, he pulled her out in one motion.

Lupe went straight to Chunk. She slapped him across the face. He punched her in the stomach, knocking the wind out of her, and causing her to collapse on the cement apron.

Chiba, the drug boss from Rio, stepped forward. He was powerfully built with muscles showing from his designer t-shirt. He placed himself between DeLuna and Lupe as Carlos also stepped in to help Lupe up. Chiba put his hand on Chunk's elbow and led him to the cabana housing the poolside bar.

Carlos guided Lupe toward the house, "Lupe, please, he's a little high."

"And I'm a little insane. I could kill that pig," Lupe said glaring over her shoulder in DeLuna's direction.

Chunk overheard the statement and started to turn. "My friend," Chiba said, "Tell me about how to keep our enemies out of our business."

# 17

Estephan aligned the three students in a triangle. Two women were facing a wall of windows overlooking the Capibaribe River; the third woman faced a wall of bricks as she took long brush strokes with a mixed blue/green pigment to capture the bird's extended tail feathers. Puckerlips, the painting, was nearing birth.

When he had completed the first of his two morning "visits of encouragement," as he liked to call them, Estephan worked for a while on his own painting. It was difficult, and he kept it from the others. He was working on "a kiss," trying to capture a view of a kiss; the moment when lips, with intense human compassion behind them, actually create a kiss. The reds were not right; he needed new colors, a new aspect, a small pout. He mixed paints cautiously, then frustrated, tested them over and over on his pallet, on a board. After a time, he put his pallet and brushes down.

Estephan sat on the stool beside his easel and began strumming on his guitar a song the women all knew. "Siboney," the song of Cuba, was known and loved in the music world that is Brazil. Estephan began humming the words, accompanying himself. Soon Lupe began to sing and was joined by the other two fledgling artists who were at work in this lesson.

It was the way Estephan ended every painting session in his studio. He would pick an obscure song, but one that everyone knew from their life in this music capital of the universe. It was always a rhythmic ballad. It always left the painters in a good mood even if their work did not progress as they hoped during that session.

The other two painters packed up, cleaned brushes and left with a flicker of a knowing smile to each other that Lupe was staying after class—again.

Estephan continued playing his guitar, and Lupe walked behind him. She put her arm around Estephan's back and leaned her head onto his shoulder.

"I am at peace here," she said softly

**********

The following week at Lupe's next class, she found Estephan busy in a corner of the studio, next to the window overlooking the Capibaribe River, a mile before it flows into the Atlantic Ocean. Estephan was big on light, and the morning light flooded in from the four large east-facing windows.

"Estephan, are you painting the river?" Lupe asked as she approached, about to peek around the canvas.

He pulled the easel to block her view. "No, you may not see it yet, my dear," he smiled.

"Come on, just a peek," and she approached from the side again.

"No, Lupe," he said pulling the easel he was working at away from her gaze. "I don't want you to see all the rules I'm breaking."

"What rules?"

"The way I teach you to paint is not the way I paint," he said, trying to distract her prying eyes.

"But, I've never seen you paint anything. Please?" she smiled.

"Soon. When I'm done. Will that be alright?" he pleaded.

The other students had not arrived yet, and the impetuous Lupe bent forward and kissed Estephan a second time. It caught him by surprise, but he quickly moved forward and they began a long tender kiss. He was overjoyed. Again, he thought. Again!

Their arms wrapped around each other; their lips desperately searching each other out. She stroked his thinning hair softly. Lupe was heating up quickly; she was catching fire. What did this mean?

120

Never before had she lit up like this. She was excited, this feeling; there was meaning without understanding what it meant. She was confused, deliriously.

And then it ended. They were interrupted by the sound of a door being pulled open in the main studio. One of the other students had arrived.

**********

Later, as Estephan made his rounds encouraging each of the students, he paused behind Lupe. "And how is it you feel this way, Estephan?" he said to himself. How is this lovely young woman awakening senses that for so long have been dormant. He could smell her from five feet away; she wore a distinctive perfume. He wanted to take those five steps, spin her around and kiss her lips. The hell with the other students, he laughed to himself. This is important; she makes me feel important, again. There was a bravado bursting forward underneath, in his brain. That was the young Estephan; the "young Brazilian Picasso" they called him. Where had he been for so long. I'll tell you where: making a living, putting food on the table, paying rent, paying bus fare, paying for the studio. The young Brazilian Picasso had been sat on by the weight of the world, by the weight of his conscience, of his responsibilities to his wife. And now this, the boy who lived in the man was here; he'd come out.

Estephan did not interrupt his students as they painted; he simply came up from behind, stood for several minutes watching and then whispered some guidance, some encouragement.

As he watched her from behind, he noticed she had slipped out of her sandals. She stood barefoot painting Puckerlips. He wanted to stroke the bottoms of her feet, see the flash of her infectious smile and hear the throaty laughter of this young woman.

*******

Two weeks later time was up at the end of another class and the other students left; Lupe stayed. Estephan continued working on his

121

painting, absorbed, unaware that the others had gone. Lupe came to the area of the studio he had been working in.

"May I see it now; is it nearly finished?"

"Lupe, no, not yet," Estephan looked at her from around the canvas. It was if he was peeking at her, and he smiled.

"You seem like a little boy, looking out from behind your painting," Lupe laughed.

"I feel like a little boy when I am around you," he said as he placed his brush on the edge of the easel and stepped out from behind the painting.

Lupe went to him and embraced him. They stood together holding each other. There was a fit here—two people with a space in their hearts finding a partner capable of fulfilling the void, the emptiness. In that embrace everything changed; what had been unsaid was now known.

# 18

Chunk sat alone on the beach. This was his release. He was dressed only in shorts. Many years had passed since a young Juan DeLuna sat alone in poverty on this same beach. Everything was the same, all these years later.

"Except poverty. I'm not poor anymore," he said to no one.

He smiled, satisfied with how he had improved the life of the young boy.

This day was Wednesday—Chunk's day—no business, no meetings. Monday, Tuesday, Thursday, and Friday he worked at his business. Saturday and Sunday were to spend at home with Lupe. Wednesday, "My day," he spoke aloud, again.

A walker along the beach looked at Chunk and said, "Ola, bom dia," believing Chunk had said "Nice Day."

Chunk nodded, and raised his right arm in acknowledgement.

On Wednesdays, Chunk drove his Austin Martin barefoot from his Recife oceanfront home to Boa Viagem beach. He would run along this beach of his youth barefoot and spend the rest of the day siting on the sand talking to strangers or buying beef snacks or coco frios from the beach side stands he and his beach kings used to rob.

On these days he would flirt with girls, who for the most part were horrified by the sight of the powerfully built but short, ugly man. A penguin in human skin. A physical oxymoron. Occasionally an innocent from the public housing projects would make the

123

mistake of listening to his advances, accept his invitation for a ride in his car and find herself pinned beneath Chunk, under a pier or in an hourly rental hotel by the Capibaribe River, the part away from the ocean that was still old and run down.

This freedom, these Wednesdays, were refreshing for DeLuna. The pressures of his business subsided and Lupe's needs evaporated. Yet, DeLuna found that as Lupe spent more time with her art classes and painting she tended not to pester him so much. Chunk actually liked a number of her paintings and felt Lupe had much talent. He vowed as she progressed he would help her get her art properly recognized.

The sun would heat the earth around him to ninety-five degrees this Wednesday, and DeLuna would take several long swims in the ocean to cool off.

"One day I will swim all the way to Noronha," he said wading out of the water as waves smacked him in the back. He could hear Lupe now speaking of Noronha, the tropical paradise of islands four hundred miles to the east, "Estephan says it has the clearest ocean water in the world, and I could paint the fish as they swim close to shore," Lupe kept reminding Chunk and asking him to take her there so she could paint.

"Fuck Estephan," Chunk said as he sat back down in the sand. "He'd better stick to his painting."

Chunk laid back, his powerful hands behind his head. He drifted off, hearing the forro music of northeast Brazil playing in his brain from the night before. He had been at the feast of Sao Juan and Sao Pedro and the people of Olinda celebrated. There was no killing last night, no drug deals, no magistrates to bribe, just Chunk and Lupe with Raphael and Lupe's younger sister, Antoinette. They flowed like lava, all the people of Olinda, down the cobblestone streets to the sea. Earlier in the evening, the restaurants of this early colonial town were overflowing with diners. At precisely 10 p.m. the bell from Sao Pedro Church began pealing. Three bands took up positions at various locations along the "lava" route. Olindians left the restaurants and began dancing in the streets to music of the bands: the samba band was at the front of the parade, halfway down the winding road; the salsa band took up its position outside the restaurant that DeLuna had been eating at. Chunk wanted to get in line to dance behind the salsa band, but Lupe asked to wait for the forro band, which was near the end. Chunk was OK with that as he liked dancing to forro; he liked the accordions and the fast pace.

Now in his sleep on the beach, DeLuna could see the serpentine route the people were taking down to the beach. After thirty minutes the snake of people reached the sea as the three bands spread out along the shore and continued playing. Lupe danced with Raphael at the edge of the water, and Chunk danced with Lupe's sister, whom he was growing quite fond of.

In his dream now, he was laughing as they danced. He put his hand on Antoinette's rear and pulled her closer to him. Lupe saw him and laughed as she wrapped both arms around Raphael and kissed him.

Chunk had seen that and bristled in his slumber in the sand. He found himself dreaming he was back on that bridge so long ago when he first met Raphael with his infected eye. Now he was holding Raphael down on the bridge, gouging his eye out with one hand as he strangled him with the other. The music of the forro band kept playing in his head, and he shuttered awake on the beach.

"What was that? Two dreams at once?" DeLuna wondered how that was possible. He never remembered something like that before. He laughed at his imagined dreams. Raphael would never betray him with Lupe. He would kill Raphael if he did. On the other hand, he thought, he found Antoinette's tight rear enchanting. That part of the dream was real and he thought out of sight of Lupe and Raphael. He wondered if Lupe would ever betray him. He was too good to Lupe; she would never do that.

Chunk rose from the sand and went for another swim. He swam a half mile down the beach, came out of the water and shook himself off. He walked up to a stand where he was friends with the owner and asked for a beer. They exchanged small talk. Chunk walked away with the beer without paying for it. It was a price of his friendship; things he wanted, small or large, he took.

Back in the sand, in the same area he had been sitting earlier, he drank his beer. He looked out at the ocean. His mind replayed the previous day. He and Raphael picked Antoinette up from the shop she worked at inside Sao Pedro Church. The church was at the center of a large square on a plateau atop Olinda. The square was surrounded by shops with a park beside the church. They were early, and Raphael parked his car. He and Chunk walked among the old Indian women siting on the edge of the park sewing, weaving and selling their delicate handmade lace wares: table cloths, napkins, and curtains.

Chunk purchased two intricately designed table cloths for Lupe. She had grown to like frilly, delicate things. As they walked into the Church of Sao Pedro, Chunk could see Antoinette in the church shop. Chunk dipped his fingers in the holy water and blessed himself.

Raphael was surprised by this, "Chunk, are you becoming holy?"

"No, it's for Antoinette."

Playfully, Raphael said to Chunk, "You already have her sister. Antoinette is mine."

Chunk growled at Raphael.

Antoinette called out. "I'll just be a minute," she said and began closing up the shop.

"You're on a date with Antoinette, to keep her company, with Lupe and me. Don't get any ideas. She's not your type," Chunk said.

Raphael was downcast. He thought Antoinette was a decent, very pretty girl. He sensed the coldness of Chunk though and felt Chunk had designs on Antoinette. What could he, Raphael, do about that?

When Antoinette came out, the three drove the two blocks down to the restaurant, Pumpkins, where they met Lupe who had been dropped off by a friend. The owner, another of Chunk's long-time "friends," welcomed him warmly in the packed house. He took DeLuna's party through an arch to a balcony table that looked out over the red and green terra cotta roofs of Olinda. The roofs made a patchwork quilt to the sea while palm trees lined the streets and their fronds blew in the evening sea breeze.

Pumpkins specialty was pumpkins. This night was the feast of Sao Pedro and Sao Paulo, a significant Catholic holy day for mostly Catholic Brazil. When the owner came to take their orders, Chunk ordered for all four. "Mango and shrimp." The owner smiled; this was the restaurant's classic dish. Mango and shrimp in a hollowed-out pumpkin, simmering for an hour. "The best choice in Olinda, Mr. DeLuna," he said to Chunk, pleased with the choice, but knowing he would not be paid for the meal. He did not mind too much; DeLuna did not take advantage of him, he just took. He expected there was something to be gained in return, but he could never figure it out. And he was not about to ask DeLuna for anything.

They ate and drank, and then they drank some more. At 10 p.m. when the church bells began ringing, the restaurant door flew open and the diners, now revelers, spilled out into the streets. They sang and they danced and the bands led them like pied pipers down to the sea in the moonlight. DeLuna's hand had found Antoinette's tight rear as they swayed in the street.

In the sand, finishing off his bottle of beer, DeLuna smiled thinking of the fun he had the night before, thinking of how he would love to take Antoinette under the pier.

# 19

Several months had gone by and Lupe's progress as a painter grew under the increasingly focused tutelage of Estephan Kelly. Their weekly sessions had come to contain two parts. One part was painting instruction with others in a class. The second part, once the other student artists had left, was individual instruction followed by intimacy.

Late on one such afternoon, Lupe lay naked in Estephan's arms, weeping. They made a huge leap from an embrace in the studio to the bed Estephan kept in the back room of the studio. This day they had made love—for hours. As the sun moved lower in the sky, Lupe was spent and full. No man had ever touched her so gently or caressed her so long. He met her with long passionate, searching kisses that found an eager starving mate.

Ten years after moving in with Chunk DeLuna, twelve years after losing her virginity, twenty-seven-year-old Lupe Monserrat discovered love. Her teacher, her kind, soulful, artistic mentor, took her to a place in her soul she was unaware of.

It was that third kiss that sent her to bed with Estephan—the one that followed the long embrace behind the painting Lupe found Estephan furiously working on, the one that pictured a kiss. A kiss of Lupe and Estephan's.

As they held each other in that embrace, Estephan pictured the painting; he saw her lips, saw the beauty of them. He felt their softness in his mind; he could smell Lupe as he envisioned the kiss.

Then he moved his lips to hers. He was creating the kiss he was painting. He felt it. It was not just a painting, it was real, it was her lips and the power, the feeling behind them that flowed forward. He now knew he would be able to complete the painting of the kiss, and he stopped worrying about the painting, stopped worrying what was driving the needs of Lupe.

They had not said a word for a long time. There was much searching and discovery in the strength of the drive from each body. The tired air conditioning unit in this old industrial building added to the intensity of their love making. Sweat poured from them as they lay on the damp sheet.

"What do you want from life, Estephan?" Lupe asked after a time, quite sincerely. As he heard the question, he realized that Lupe did not see a sixty-seven-year-old man but someone else. He mattered, maybe not for long, maybe not forever with her, but right now Estephan Kelly mattered.

"If God was truly good, he would make me twenty-seven again so I could walk with you through life," and he laughed.

Lupe looked at him. She thought he might be laughing at her. "No, no Lupe. I am not trying to be funny at your expense," he said, pulling her close with his right arm that cradled her head and shoulder. "This is such a great gift. Such a great cruel gift that God has given me, I am saddened that it will not last beyond today."

"Estephan, my dear. Why not?" the young woman said. She raised her head, propping it with the palm of her hand, elbow bent into the sheet.

"Look at us. Lupe you are beautiful, a goddess. I am an older man—not an old man, but older. Old enough to know that dreams are not real."

"We are not a dream. Do you think of me as a dream?" she questioned him.

"Yes, my dear, my dear love. You are a dream. You are what men dream of when their lives are plain, burdensome and ending. You are what old men call hope."

Lupe sat up, crisscrossed her legs in her nakedness. This sight, this position she assumed in her nakedness, brought a broad smile to

Estephan's face. "What," she said. "Oh, men. You are the same that way," and she laughed. Lupe leaned forward and turned his face with both of her hands so that she was facing him from a distance of four inches. "This is me, Estephan. Look at me. I am not a dream."

"I am looking," he smiled, and they both laughed lustily.

"You have touched me, Estephan. You have filled me. You have given me confidence, taught me. You have encouraged me; your whispers have reached my soul. I want you to continue to teach me."

"Of course I will continue to teach you."

"You are not listening. Not painting. Life. I want to be in your life, and I want you to always be in my life."

"Yes, Lupe. I know what you mean. And I do think I understand what you mean now. I have those same feelings. I will confess there is a faint echo of a time long ago when I felt something similar."

"For your wife?"

"Yes," he paused. "She is blameless in life. A sweet soul who has stayed by my side through the worst. Worse than you can imagine."

"Try me, I have a vivid imagination and have not been a wallflower in the house of misery."

"Ah, my dear. There was a time," and Estephan's gaze went back years. He could see himself then; a light came across his face.

"What time? Who were you then?"

"I was the one. The one every painter wants to be."

"Such modesty," she poked with a laugh.

"You asked," he said, back from the past. "I was competent— had great skill. They said it, not me."

"Who."

"The critics. My teachers. "He was born to paint," "The Brazilian Picasso.""

"I believe it," she said. "I have seen your paintings."

"You've seen a few. Not the ones in the private galleries, not the ones stolen from me. The leeches took my soul. Bastards took everything I created. My work should be in museums—it is not."

She saw anger and resentment flash across the face of her gentle teacher. "I'm not following you. Who took your work?"

130

"My benefactors," he said sarcastically, with a snarl. "Came to the studio, this studio. Bought everything I created."

"That's good, isn't it, Estephan?" Lupe asked, confused by the seeming conflict.

"Good in that people recognized my work. Bad that I needed the money, wouldn't get an agent or manager, and I let everything go for nothing."

"What's nothing?"

"Nothing. Pennies. You've heard starving artist jokes?" he asked.

"Yes," Lupe answered meekly.

"Starving artist with family. I could never get ahead. The critics came to our shows, wrote raves about what they saw. Then the buyers showed up. But they weren't the ones I needed. These were the middlemen, not patrons. Leeches preying on the needs of the artist. Buying, bargaining for next to nothing. Selling works into the hands of buyers we never knew."

"Do I miss your meaning here?"

"Lupe, there is recreational painting, which is where we come together. An individual seeking to grow a new talent—you. An old hack teacher eking out a living—me. Recreational painting."

Lupe did not take offense. She understood and laughed. "At least I understand where I stand."

"No offense."

"No," she replied. "But now tell me what is the other form."

"The artist. The artiste! The god with golden palette. Me," and after a pause, "Then."

"But aren't these same people still buying your paintings?" Lupe asked.

"No. I won't sell them to the bastards."

"Why not?"

"The paintings disappear. People have no idea what they're buying. They hang my beauties on the walls of their homes, and they have no idea of the value, of the work that went into it. They have no idea of the genius behind the work."

"My, my. The humility grows," Lupe said soothingly, as she could see the anguish that had put the crevices in his brow and cheeks.

"One of the most important things a good artist must do is cultivate sponsors. Sponsors with taste, deep pockets and a willingness to continue with an artist over decades. All the great artists had those sponsors. It is the only reason you know who they are today. Their backers supported them, promoted them and bought their works. But it wasn't a charity. If the great artist and his sponsor work well together then the sponsors' purchases will grow in value. That painting he paid one thousand dollars for thirty years ago could be worth five or ten million today."

"What?" Lupe exclaimed. "You're kidding me. But you mean someone like Picasso himself? Yes."

"Yes, but hundreds of very capable artists could also be seeing their works appreciate in that same way," then looking up at Lupe in her nakedness, he reached for her and pulled her back down on the bed with him.

They laid silent for a time then Lupe asked, "So what about your paintings. Do you still paint to earn money? Or are you just teaching?"

"I teach to earn money. I paint for love; I no longer sell my work."

"What do you do with what you paint?" she asked.

"I keep them."

"Where," she asked, and thinking, "I've only seen a few on the walls."

Estephan stood up naked. He was lean but had a stronger frame than it seemed when he had clothes on and except for a slight stoop forward, looked younger than his years. He reached down and took Lupe's hand. "Come with me."

As the sun was setting on the other side of the studio, Estephan led Lupe. They walked in their nakedness to a door in a darkened corner of the bedroom. He opened the door and put his hand up to stop her from advancing. He entered through the door and switched lights on.

"Come in."

Lupe Monserrat entered a cavernous room, equal in size to Estephan's entire studio. Rows of wood structures held paintings, one leaning on another until they were braced by a wooden separator. She walked in. Her mouth was open, and she raised her hand to stop sound from escaping. She walked down one aisle looking at painting after painting. Estephan waited at the end of the aisle. Lupe came back up another aisle. Hundreds of paintings stood at attention in their racks, down aisle after aisle.

"These are not yours. You keep other artists' paintings here also."

"Only mine. The Brazilian Picasso," he bowed naked, laughing.

"No, Estephan. This is enormous," she said and proceeded to pull out one painting, then another, examining each. She continued to do this walking naked along Estephan's rows of art. They were segmented by form, genre. Hundreds of geometric forms of half-shaped angular bodies in earth tones, then portraits—big, regal portraits of people without a penny. Portraits of the street people of Recife wrapped in velvet for the sitting: poor mulatto faces; black, black Bahians; proud Castilian or Neapolitan noses; long arrogant Arab faces with beards. Then came the landscapes: the jungle, the city, even Brasilia, in Picasso motifs. There was even an early model of the giant jungle mural in the studio.

"I see," Lupe said, saddened by what she now grasped. "Oh my sweet, sweet Estephan. They did this to you. They kept you from the world," she embraced him.

Estephan took a deep, exhausted breath. He tilted his head and laid it on Lupe's shoulder. No soul had ever set foot in his store room. For thirty years he had been stockpiling all of his paintings; he had retreated from the world that stole from him.

# 20

It was finished! Long lush feathers. Blue on the wings, green along the back. Short plush red feathers on the breast. A blue head with yellow around the ears. Lupe's painting of Puckerlips the parrot was finished.

With great formality, Lupe was to introduce the two Puckerlips to the assembled guests who had gathered in the salon of her home for the occasion. Chunk DeLuna spared no expense for Lupe's artistic coming out. White jacketed waiters carried trays of hors d'oeuvres; waiters in red jackets offered champagne and wine. Around the room hung twelve large works of art by Lupe Monserrat. In the center of the room, with a drape over it, was her pride, an effort that took fully seven months. Lupe completed one work after another during her first eighteen months of painting, but it was the painting of her pet parrot, Puckerlips, that consumed her. First done several times in smaller scale and now this large work, fully eight feet tall, was ready for viewing.

For Estephan Kelly, Lupe was the ideal art student. She did not miss class, was always on time, stayed after class continuing to work, and she worked hard. She listened to her mentor and practiced what he taught. But most of all, Estephan saw she had talent.

And now here they were. A hundred or so assembled guests. A mix of Recifeian society, a very broad mix. Estephan of course was there at Lupe's insistence, despite DeLuna's objection. Chunk hated

Estephan. They had only met twice, but it was not the physical meeting that turned DeLuna off on the teacher. It was DeLuna's lunacy: anyone who had an influence on Lupe was a threat to DeLuna. Jealously boiled under his skin every moment.

"He can't come," DeLuna had said while he and Lupe were planning the party, sorting through who to invite. "The senators will be here. Business leaders from the city. Many of my good customers. He's riff raff. He doesn't belong."

"You're calling Estephan riff raff!" Lupe shrieked. "You!"

While DeLuna dominated Lupe Monserrat, she would not be dominated. He would boss people around; he would scream at them. He would even beat them into submission. He did these same things to Lupe. He was always dominating her. Her fierce grasp on her own life would not allow Chunk to dominate her.

"Fuck you, Chunk!" she shrieked after he slapped her on the cheek. "He's coming or I'll have my own party without your gang."

"You bitch," he said slapping her again. He walked away. The guest list was complete.

Invited of course were the Reis da Praia, the four original beach kings, the heart of DeLuna's criminal empire. Now, years into the larger criminal enterprise they were installed in various positions inside CDL Enterprisa with Carlos as the CEO of CDL Cement and Construction.

The party's guests were all couples but for three or four singles. If there were fifty men, there were fifty spouses. The men, whether senator, business leader, or drug dealer, were all criminals. Involvement with DeLuna meant you were a criminal. There was just no way you would ever involve yourself with this subspecies. You expected something: a pay-off, a steady flow of drugs, a kickback, a gambling debt reduced, or a woman; it was the way CDL operated.

There was one honest man this night; it was Estephan Kelly. He came by himself. Lupe was not in the salon as Kelly walked from painting to painting admiring the work of his pupil, his inamorata, the love that was bringing life to his soul.

In the twenty-five years Kelly had been teaching, there were several students who possessed artistic gifts. There were even another two or three who had the drive to produce big works. None of them possessed both. Just Lupe, she had both talent and drive. The paintings around the room were proof: large works of nature, still lifes, even a portrait. But the gathering would soon see the extent of her talent: an eight-foot-tall painting of Puckerlips. Lupe had successfully modeled the painting in an earlier three-foot primer. Now the genius was about to be shared with the assembly.

Applause broke out as Lupe entered the room. She had not expected that and lowered her head. Her cheeks, red with rouge, became crimson.

She walked to the draped master work of her beloved bird. The guests moved in closer, like an accordion folding up. Lupe motioned Estephan to come stand beside her.

DeLuna was ignored. He boiled inside and came out of the crowd to stand beside Lupe. What the guests were facing was DeLuna, Lupe, the painting, and Estephan.

"Ladies and gentlemen," Lupe began and turned her back to DeLuna as she looked at Estephan Kelly. "My instructor, Mr. Estephan Kelly, has taken extraordinary interest in my development as a painter, and I will be forever grateful. I thank him from the bottom of my heart."

DeLuna's frame began pulsating. His jealously screamed inside. The heat was building.

"Estephan, dear, would you please help me unveil Puckerlips."

"Estephan, dear," the words escaped DeLuna's tightly clenched jaw.

Kelly smiled, reached and tugged gently at the purple velvet drape that fell revealing the gigantic, colorful bird. A spotlight was shining on the painting, and it enhanced the colors. Brush strokes were revealed in the light. The guests erupted in applause. It was a work of art. The scale. The stunning colors all coming together to make a bird unlike any of them had seen before. Even a personality showed through in the glint in the big bird's eye—a speck of white positioned just right in a round black eye ball. It was a true likeness of the real bird who sat perched in his cage opposite his portrait, between the sets of French doors leading to the patio.

Later after dinner when the guests reassembled in the salon, Lupe had two of the waiters move Puckerlip's cage next to the painting.

The guests began mingling by the two birds. "Beautiful," "amazing likeness," and "brilliant colors match him perfectly," were comments being spoken. Chunk DeLuna stood nearby with Carlos at his side.

"Chunk, Lupe has created a masterpiece," Carlos said and went on more effusively, and for him, truthfully, "Chunk, it's brilliant."

"It's a fucking painting, a painting of a bird," DeLuna fumed. "I don't get it. What's everyone getting excited about."

"Come on, Chunk. Be happy for her. She really worked hard on this."

"Carlos, it's a fucking bird," DeLuna said, a little too loud. Puckerlips cranked his head to the side and spied DeLuna.

"Fuck you, Chunk," the bird screeched, one of the phrases Lupe had taught him after Chunk beat her.

Guests sanding nearby broke into hysterical laughter as they turned and looked at DeLuna. Chunk got red, smiled tightly and said, "Stupid bird," taking a step forward to interdict the bird.

"Fuck you, Chunk," Puckerlips screeched again, jumping to the edge of his cage grabbing an outside bar with his claws. DeLuna stepped forward and smashed his hand against the cage as the bird hopped back.

"Chunk, let's get a drink," Carlos said, guiding DeLuna away from an embarrassing situation that was not going to improve.

"I'll kill that fucker someday," DeLuna grumbled out of earshot of the still giggling guests.

*********

The next morning was a glorious day. Lupe bounded out of bed, still in the glow of the previous evening. She leaned over towards DeLuna, "Come on, Chunk. Let's go to the beach."

DeLuna was still sleepy from staying up too late drinking with Carlos, Raphael, Pedro, and Paco by the pool after the guests and their wives had left. "Alright," he moaned.

"I'm going down to the salon to look at the paintings in the morning light; come with me."

"I'll be along; you go," DeLuna said as he turned over in bed.

A minute later DeLuna heard a scream so loud it reminded him of someone being tortured, someone in fact he may have tortured. He rose up and ran to the top of the stairs that overlooked the salon. Beneath him on the marble floor lay Lupe Monserrat crying, sobbing uncontrollably. Above her on the wall was the painting of Puckerlips. The bird's head had been severed from its body. It had been slashed repeatedly. It was destroyed.

She sensed DeLuna above on the second floor landing. "You did this. You lousy prick. You destroyed my painting," Lupe screamed through her crying.

DeLuna rushed downstairs, flew to Lupe's side on the floor.

"No, no, Lupe," he pleaded. "I would never do this."

"You did it," she swung at him from her prone position but missed.

"No, Lupe," he said again. "I did not. But I will find out who did this. And I will kill him," he said emphatically.

Lupe looked at him. She was convinced she heard conviction. The anger that came from DeLuna was real. She started to believe, "Maybe he didn't do it."

That same afternoon, when Lupe came downstairs after a nap from her darkened bedroom, she cried again for her work. The painting she had put so much love into.

A short time later DeLuna walked in with a rope around the neck of a man. Chunk had two of his gang members beside him. DeLuna tugged on the rope pulling the man in before Lupe as if he were an animal.

"What did you do," DeLuna said moving into the man's personal space, stopping inches from his face. The man was shaking, crying. He was in his mid to late twenties.

"Tell the lady what you did," DeLuna said, yanking on the noose around his neck.

"I was a waiter at the party last night."

"Go on," DeLuna urged.

"And when it ended, when we were cleaning up, I saw the painting. You were out beside the pool drinking with some men." He paused here, DeLuna nodded in Lupe's direction, indicating that he should go on.

"I had been looking at the painting of the bird all night. It was bothering me," he cried louder.

"Go on, you bastard."

"So I killed it. I slashed it, carved it up," his confession was a tight throated plea. "I did not like it," he said looking at Lupe and then at DeLuna.

DeLuna pulled a gun from underneath his shirt. The waiter who confessed to slashing the painting pulled back, alarmed at seeing the gun. DeLuna pulled on the rope, yanking the man's neck, pulling him closer. Then he shot him. The man fell to the floor, dead, in front of Lupe.

Lupe reeled back in horror at the sight. Now she knew it was DeLuna who had carved up her painting of the bird.

# PART

4

# 21

*News Brazil—All Media*

*Silvina Arancha*

*February 12, 2015*

*Manaus*

*The 2016 Olympic organizing committee said last Thursday that Brazil's Manaus Stadium will host matches for the Rio Games, subject to the approval of FIFA, world soccer's governing body.*

*"Nothing is more emblematic than Amazonia," said the organizing committee chairman. He said the Games of Brazil must be inclusive of all of Brazil, not just Rio, the host city.*

*In January FIFA had expressed concern that the four stadiums proposed for Olympic soccer would stand up to multiple use in the Olympics. Brazil proposed using two more stadiums for soccer, including Manaus.*

*FIFA has taken the recommendation under advisement. There was concern, however, from last year's World Cup soccer matches in Manaus that the distance from the venues was too great. Manaus and Rio are about eighteen hundred miles apart. Its location in the heart of the Amazon rain forest also brought complaints from European soccer teams over the high humidity.*

*There will be more than high humidity if the $300 million stadium becomes a white elephant. After all, there was considerable controversy and street protests over the need for this stadium in a city with a level four soccer club that averages 350 paying customers at each match.*

**\*\*\*\*\*\*\*\*\***

*News Brazil—All Media*

*Silvina Arancha*

*February 13, 2015*

*Manaus*

*FIFA, world soccer's governing body, said it "does not consider Manaus as a suitable first option" to host Olympic soccer.*

*FIFA's quick and negative reaction to Manaus appears to have surprised Brazil's Olympic committee. Brazil is trying to "integrate all of Brazil," into the Olympic games and only yesterday had submitted Manaus as one of six sites to host soccer.*

*Next month when FIFA's Olympic committee meets, Brazil's proposal will be discussed. FIFA stated they prefer the games be played closer to the host city of Rio.*

*To say FIFA's objection throws a wrench into the country's plans is putting it mildly. Sources have said the President of Brazil is furious at FIFA's attempt to dictate to Brazil.*

## March 8, 2015

"Mr. DeLuna," Bruno Ferreira, the deputy head of the Brazil Olympic Committee, began from behind his large mahogany desk, "we need your help."

Chunk DeLuna sat in the rich leather chair on the other side of the desk. His feet did not touch the floor, and that bothered him as anything that called attention to his small height bothered him. Still, on this morning, the deputy head of the Brazilian Olympic Committee had called him in. The committee was pleased with the work DeLuna's firm, CDL Enterprisa, had done in building the Manaus Olympic Stadium. Built in the middle of the Amazon jungle, the work was arduous with almost insurmountable obstacles of getting all the materials to the site. The local Manaus Project Manager and the overall Olympic Project Manager had been effusive in their praise of CDL. Of all the Olympic venues, being built by five other companies similar to CDL, it was only DeLuna's that was constantly on time at each milestone and it was only DeLuna's that finished ahead of schedule. The site had been successfully used in the 2014 World Cup soccer matches and got widespread praise, except for the unbelievable heat and humidity in the jungle, which were beyond CDL's control.

In fact, the site even survived what was now called a small earthquake, an imperceptible shake that occurred two months after the World Cup and which resulted in nothing more than a two-foot-long crack along the top of the southeast wall.

In the weeks after the "shake," geologists and engineers reaffirmed the safety of the stadium and attributed it to a settling of the earth after creating an enormous fifty-two thousand seat stadium.

"Yes, Mr. Ferreira, anything I can do to help, anything at all," DeLuna replied. He was quite sincere in that, since being awarded the contract to build this particular Olympic stadium elevated DeLuna. It took him from the petty criminal and gangster, to cement manufacturer, to major construction firm.

"There's a problem with Manaus," Bruno Ferreira said.

DeLuna sat up, the minor earthquake that had occurred immediately flashed in his mind.

"FIFA, the World Cup Soccer governing body does not want to hold any Olympic soccer games in Manaus," Ferreira went on.

DeLuna was dumbstruck. He looked at Carlos who was seated silently beside him. Carlos shrugged his shoulders upward, a question mark on his face.

"I don't understand," DeLuna said. "Isn't that why it was built."

"Yes, Mr. DeLuna. That is correct—the Olympics and the World Cup."

"Then what gives?"

"They don't like the distance between Rio, where most matches will be played, and Manaus. They said there were a lot of complaints about the heat in Amazonia during the World Cup. The Europeans complained about the humidity in the jungle."

"What do they want?" a practical DeLuna chimed in. He knew everyone wanted something.

"That's where I hope you can help us," Ferreira said, now shifting uncomfortably behind his desk. "Mr. Hugo Ribeiro, our Olympic Project manager, has spoken repeatedly, very highly of you. Not only of your company's capability but of your personal ability to get things done."

DeLuna could see the discomfort in Ferreira. He had gone to university, dealt with Brazilian political royalty his whole life. Ferreira had been personally selected by the President of Brazil to be second in command to head up the Olympic Committee. He had no need of a man with the capabilities of DeLuna until now. Chunk understood what Ferreira was saying.

"Mr. Ribeiro is a good man. You are well served with him, and I thank him for his confidence," DeLuna smiled. It was Ribeiro who owed his Olympic Project Manager job to DeLuna. And it was Ribeiro who was able to get CDL Enterprisa into the final bidding process for Manaus. It was a debt he paid to DeLuna. It covered his gambling, prostitution and drug debts. He was one of DeLuna's full service customers and whose patronage of CDL services DeLuna personally tracked. It was Carlos though who saw it was important for Ribeiro to go through rehab if he was to succeed in his project management job, which was a vital concern for CDL since the value of the potential for the contract was over $200 million and growing. As the original bidding process began, Carlos coached Chunk on the value of having an insider in the Olympic bidding process. Carlos, from his database of highly skilled professionals who used CDL services, found Ribeiro and together the three, Carlos, Chunk and Ribeiro, outlined a plan to clean up the competent and professional engineer that Ribeiro was and would be again. It was men like Ribeiro who would continue on DeLuna's books to move CDL more and more into the legitimate business economy in Brazil.

"Who is it that has the decision making power to put Olympic Soccer in Manaus," Carlos asked, finally speaking from his contemplative roost.

DeLuna could see Carlos' wheels already turning. DeLuna looked back at Ferreira.

"Two people, really. FIFA's president and his right-hand man for our Olympics. We've seen the FIFA president follow the recommendation of Flavio Melo several times lately."

"And when will this final decision be made," DeLuna asked.

"Within the next two weeks. There is no time to lose. The president of our county has even been stalemated so far. She was told she would be advised in due time. She is furious and insulted. Soccer is our national sport. It is why we live. We must be able to determine the venues and show our county to the world."

DeLuna stood up. "I am sorry for your troubles in these matters; our interests are aligned. My associate and I will begin on this immediately. You have my assurances that no stone will be left unturned. Olympic soccer will be played in Manaus."

As Carlos stood up the men shook hands. "Thank you Mr. DeLuna," Ferreira concluded.

# 22

Two days later the stones were being unturned. A video attachment accompanied an e-mail to Flavio Melo, assistant to the President of FIFA. One half hour later a phone call came into his office. On the other end of the line was Angel Pagan, DeLuna's enforcer for the nefarious parts of the CDL empire.

"Sir, you have received my e-mail and seen the attachment?" the voice of Pagan asked coldly.

"I have. Please," Melo raised his voice, pleading. "Please, do not hurt him."

"That all depends on you," the kidnapper said. Melo recognized a Spanish accent on the man speaking Portuguese to him.

"He is a wonderful son. My first born. He is ...," Melo started to cry. "Is he alright?"

"He's fine. And he will stay fine as long as Manaus is one of the Olympic Soccer venues."

"That's it. That's why you kidnapped and tortured my boy?" agony apparent in Melo's every word.

"We have not tortured him yet."

"He is buried up to his neck. Rocks falling on his head. I see blood on his forehead."

"They were small stones. Your son bleeds easy," Pagan said, almost toying with the grieved father. "Are you ready to play ball," and Pagan laughed, a sick, dark laugh, "if you know what I mean."

"I cannot do that. I cannot award Manaus."

"Yes you can and yes you will in two hours. You're in Rio to make a decision on the soccer venue. Make the right decision," then Angel Pagan hung up.

Flavio Melo put his head in his hands and continued weeping. He looked at the thirty-second clip again. The setting was jungle. There was a small clearing where a hole had been dug and refilled with the obviously alive body of Melo's son, a boy of about seventeen. Only his head showed above the earth. Melo thought of how he used to bury his boy in the sand beaches of Rio. This was not the beach. From somewhere out of camera range someone was dropping or throwing stones on his son's head. It was probably that sick bastard on the phone. Melo saw his son's eyes—frightened as he had never seen them before. The eyes were pleading for the stones to stop, for this nightmare to end.

Melo picked up his phone and called FIFA's president.

************************

Two hours later Melo's phone rang. He froze. He was trembling as he pushed the talk button. "Yes?"

"I haven't heard that Manaus will be one of the Olympic venues," Angel Pagan said. "Your time is up. Do you have an answer?"

"I can't do it alone. It's the President of FIFA; it's his decision."

"You told him your situation?"

"No. I told him we must include Manaus. I said that Brazil was counting on it," Melo said.

"And he said?"

"He said 'No.' Well, 'No, unless.'"

"Unless what?" Angel demanded. "His only answer can be yes. Don't you understand the stakes here?"

"I do, I do," Melo screamed.

"Then what?" Pagan screamed back.

"He wants a consideration."

"You fuckers. Your son is about to die, and you and your boss are looking for a bribe," Pagan raged. "I'll tell you what, here's my consideration, I'll let your son live."

"He wants $100,000," Melo said, his voice quivering.

"You did not tell him I have your son. You are an idiot. You've put yourself into a position of never seeing your boy again. Why would you do that?"

"He's a hard man. He only bends to money. I do not think knowing my son is in jeopardy would affect him."

"I'm a harder man, Melo. That's too bad for your boy," Pagan said and he hung up.

"No. Don't hang up," and realizing that Pagan was gone, "Oh my God, what have I done."

Melo rose from the desk in his hotel room at the Intercontinental Hotel on Copacabana Beach. FIFA's governing body was holding its winter meeting in Rio to make its final choices for the 2016 Olympic venues for soccer.

Brazil's Olympic organizing committee provided arrangements for the five member FIFA committee and their families hoping that the hospitality would help them see the wisdom behind Brazil's wish to showcase the entire country but to no avail thus far.

Melo left his room and proceeded to the beach where FIFA's senior leadership had been basking for several days. "I need to speak to you," he said, approaching his boss.

"Get your swimsuit on; come and join us," the rotund, older man said to his assistant.

There were twenty or so members of this group: FIFA members, wives and some children.

"It is most urgent," Melo pleaded.

The FIFA President, Mr. Samuel Azevedo, acceded, seeing the anguish in Melo's face. "Alright, if you'll excuse us," he said to the others. The two talked as they walked along the sand, an odd looking couple—a middle aged man with a big gut over-hanging a skimpy Speedo and a tall, thin man dressed in a suit.

"This man holding him," Melo was saying, "he's not local, he has a Spanish accent. This is not some local prank. They will kill my son."

Suddenly, the middle aged man stopped and put his hand on the shoulder of the man in the suit. "I'm sorry, Flavio. Why didn't you tell me?"

"I thought I could handle it. Thought my recommendation would be enough," he said through tears.

"Well, not when there's money to be made," and pausing, "Excuse my cavalier attitude. Look, we can do Manaus. Call them back and tell them, yes. Just get them to let your boy go now. I'll tell the others my decision and put out an announcement first thing in the morning."

"I think it's too late."

"What? Why?"

"Before he hung up on me, the last thing he said was, "It's too late for your boy.""

"Shit!" Azevedo swore. "Then we must do this right now. I'll put an announcement out immediately."

The two hurriedly walked back toward the group. "My dear, I've got to go back to the hotel," Azevedo said. "Urgent business."

"Alright, Samuel. If you see Juliana, send her back here. I don't want her roaming too far on this beach."

With a robe on and Melo with him, Azevedo got into the elevator that whisked them to the penthouse suite.

Melo's iPhone buzzed that an email had been received. Fear struck Melo. He was terrified it would tell him his son was dead. He fumbled to pull it out of his pocket, tapped the screen

"What is it," Azevedo asked.

"This is not good," Melo said. He showed the e-mail to Azevedo. It read, "Show the fat man the video attachment." Melo tapped the screen to play the attachment.

"Daddy," Juliana Azevedo screamed from Melo's phone. She was in a bikini and a man with a mask had his arm around her neck. In his right hand he held a knife.

150

"Manaus gets Olympic soccer. One hour," the voice with the Spanish accent said.

"Jesus, what is this," Azevedo said.

"It's him," Melo said, recognizing the same voice and accent. "We have no time. Please, let's get the Manaus announcement out. It's the only thing that will satisfy these bastards."

The two men worked for ten minutes. Melo took the finished copy and powered up Azevedo's Lenovo's laptop. The message was on the airwaves within a half hour of the men leaving the beach.

That night both children were returned to the Intercontinental Hotel twenty minutes apart. Hurriedly, FIFA's governing body left Rio on an 11 p.m. flight to Sao Paulo. They just had to get to some place safe.

********

*All New Brazil—All Media*

*Silvina Arancha*

*March 11, 2015*

*Manaus*

*FIFA has withdrawn its objection to Manaus hosting Olympic soccer events next year. Soccer's governing body has agreed to Brazil's choice of the Amazon jungle city as a venue for Olympic soccer.*

*Six cities that Brazil selected and submitted for FIFA's approval will host men's and women's matches: Manaus, Rio, Belo Horizonte, Sao Paulo, Salvador, and Brasilia. These same cities hosted World Cup soccer in 2014. Earlier there had been objections to Manaus because of the distance from the host city of Rio and, not surprisingly, the humidity of the jungle.*

*The Manaus stadium, which has a capacity of fifty-two thousand and cost almost $300 million to build, ten times the original budget, has drawn complaints of waste and corruption since many* *consider it will be little used going forward. Manaus' level four soccer club draws an average of 350 paying customers to its matches.*

*Brazil was determined to have Manaus and Amazonia included in the Olympic Games and somehow found the magic to turn an increasingly arrogant FIFA to its point of view.*

*It was only last year that FIFA "persuaded" Brazil's congress to change a law that had required sports venues to offer one-half priced admissions for school children and senior citizens. The kids and seniors now must pay full price. That bit of arm twisting now seems to have been reversed as Brazil somehow found the fortitude to get Manaus included as an Olympic venue.*

# 23

News Brazil—All Media

Silvina Arancha

November 20, 2015

Manaus

Heavy spring rains suspected of helping spread Zika virus.

Sporadic outbreaks of the Zika virus are showing up in three areas of Brazil: Recife, Brasilia and Manaus. The virus, which can cause microcephaly and result in newborn babies with significantly smaller heads and diminished mental capacity, is believed to have made the journey last September from Polynesia to Brazil with World Cup participants.

This year's significantly higher rainfall, particularly in Manaus, is expected to accelerate the mosquito borne virus.

Government officials expressed no concern that this would affect next year's Olympics. "It is easily contained by spraying. Individuals in mosquito infested areas should put plenty of lotion with deet on them," said Denis Santos, Health Minister of Amazonia.

Also in the news:

*In one of those oddly Brazilian stories, a giant Arapaima, a nine-foot, 450-pound behemoth of a river fish was found a hundred miles out in the Atlantic. Scientists suspect an underground river may have dispatched him there.*

*Really? An underground river a hundred miles out to sea? Only in Brazil.*

The River Hamza was discovered in 2011 by geologists working in Brazil's interior searching for oil. What makes this river unique is that it is a twin of the Amazon and flows two miles beneath it and for nearly as long. It flows from the foothills of the Andes and empties into the Atlantic in northeast Brazil.

At Manaus, the jungle city of Amazonia, where the Amazon and Negro rivers meet, the underground River Hamza is nearly 250 miles wide, an underground ocean. Spring rains had flooded the Hamza and while the main river flows east towards the Atlantic exiting miles out in the ocean, a branch of the Hamza flows gradually upward for miles. A giant cavern had formed over millions of years above this branch of the Hamza and with the rains swelling the tributary, there was no place for the water to go but up, scraping the limestone that supports the dome above. This rogue underground branch of the Hamza then races south and over a cliff, plunging for three miles in a spectacular unseen waterfall. For eighteen hundred miles, the branch of the river races downward carving its way towards the mantle of the earth, before exiting a hundred miles out to sea under the Atlantic.

*********

The fish breached the surface; its great long gray scaly body was half as long as the approaching fishing boat.

"What the hell is that?" the young deckhand announced.

Santiago squinted, two small eyes peering out from the leather-like skin of his face into the afternoon sun, "It can't be a shark; there's no fin," he said as the boat came alongside the fish. "Whatever it is, it's dead. Get the grappling hook."

Both men worked for half an hour trying to pull the beast into the boat. "It's not going to work. We'll have to tie it to the side and hold it up with a net," Santiago said.

"We'll make a fortune with this fish," the deck hand exclaimed.

"It's not for sale. It's dead. Can't you smell it?"

"Sure I smell it. All fish stink," the deck hand replied.

"This one has a stink all its own," Santiago said to his crew, the deck hand. "I've seen one like this before. But not in the ocean."

"Not me. This is strange."

"Yes. It's a river fish a hundred miles from a river."

"How do you know?"

"Because we're a hundred miles from shore."

"I know that," the hand said, frustrated that his boss did not understand that he knew he was a hundred miles out in the south Atlantic Ocean. "How do you know it's a river fish, I mean."

"Because that's where arapaima live, in the Amazon," Santiago said, leaning over the side of the boat looking at the fish they had now secured by a net and ropes to the stern. "Come here. Tell me what you see," Santiago said pointing to the head of the fish.

"His eyes?"

"Yes."

"They're white. He's blind?"

"Was. He was blind," Santiago corrected, as he did all day long, semantically one-upping the deck hand.

"No wonder he ended up a hundred miles out to sea."

Santiago laughed, "That's a good one. He got lost. Ha, ha, ha."

The younger man laughed along with Santiago, pleased he had been able to come up with a creative thought, since Santiago was constantly on him for one thing or another.

"But there is no way he swam out here, right?"

"Right. And where he lived was dark, no light, which is why his eyes are white," Santiago scratched his head. "This is confusing."

"Why?"

"Because I think he's an air breather, he constantly comes up for air."

"Was an air breather," the deck hand said with a smile. Santiago slapped him on the back, "You got me - ha, ha, ha." Both men laughed.

*********

The fish had been dead for several days before Santiago found it; the smell told them that. When Santiago hoisted the fish up at the weigh station back on the docks in Recife, it measured eleven feet and weighed five hundred pounds. Small crowds came throughout the day and many took pictures with the fish and Santiago. One picture appeared in Recife's main newspaper the next day accompanied by the fish story. Several days later it appeared with Santiago's story in other papers throughout the country.

*********

"Did you see that fish story?" Elena Lucena, the chief scientist at the Amazon Institute, a think tank for the sustainability of the rain forest, located in the nation's capital, Brasilia, asked her colleague.

"I'm looking at it now," Rodrigo Costa, an environmental engineer, said.

"What is an arapaima doing in the middle of the ocean?" the scientist said, leaning over his shoulder. "And pretty well preserved," she added looking at the picture of the smiling fisherman Santiago standing beside the behemoth.

"There's that story a couple of years ago about the underground river, the Hamza, that supposedly empties out into the ocean, further out than the Amazon," she said, almost by way of a question.

"We did some research initially, but we're waiting for the geologists to do more work," Rodrigo replied. "At any rate that would be a stretch. The fish is a breather, so it can't live that far down."

"But you saw the part about its eyes, they were white, ergo, lives in darkness."

"You're funny when you're serious," he laughed. "The facts as we know them are too disparate to make any sense—a river two

156

miles underground, a white-eyed air breathing fish, and it shows up a hundred miles off shore."

"Anyway," Lucena said, "let's call up the geologist who originally discovered the river. His name is Hamza. See if they have come up with more on this river, no rush, but let's look deeper."

\*\*\*\*\*\*\*\*\*

*News Brazil—All Media*

*Silvina Arancha*

*February 2, 2016*

*Manaus*

*As if Brazil's challenges in preparing for the 2016 Olympics in August were not already daunting, now comes the Zika virus and it is serious.*

*Today the World Health Organization declared the Zika virus outbreak to be a global emergency. In Brazil, the country hit hardest by the outbreak, fear is spreading among pregnant women after government officials linked the virus to thousands of cases of microcephaly which results in abnormally small heads and underdeveloped brains.*

*Health Minister Marcelo Castro, a psychiatrist from Rio, said, "Eighty percent of people infected by Zika do not develop significant symptoms, so the situation is more serious than we can imagine." Castro went on to say the virus cannot be transmitted from one person to another, only by mosquitos."*

\*\*\*\*\*\*\*\*\*

Three months had gone by since Elena Lucena had asked Rodrigo Costa to look into the underground River Hamza, aptly named for its discoverer. Costa was standing in the doorway of Lucena's office.

"Got some interesting stuff on that big fish that was discovered a hundred miles out to sea," he began.

"What's up?"

"I didn't catch it in the story, but they said the fish was blind."

"White eyes, I thought you knew that," Lucena said.

"Also, what they think is the fish lived in the underground river, never saw sunlight and morphed some thousands of years ago into a sightless cousin of the arapaima."

"But it would need air."

"The geologists said there would be lots of air flowing through the cavern that the river carved," Rodrigo said. "However, they were as surprised as us that the fish was that far out to sea when it was found."

"And?" she said.

"And, since it was so well preserved they think there must have been something like a great toilet flush, sucking the thing down and out."

"See," Elena Lucena laughed, "that's what happens when you go to guys who have rocks in their heads."

"I know. It's actually funny but they did add a couple of other things that make some sense."

"Like?"

"Well, last year we had the drought and this year the rains—lots of rains up river, in the jungle, coming out of the Andes. They had been doing follow-up work, up by Manaus on the underground river flow. You know, trying to track how the Hamza flows beneath the Amazon and how closely it tracks to the Amazon. They said this year they have noticed a much stronger underground flow to the river, nothing compared to the Amazon, but still four times faster than the flow of the past three years."

"How do they account for the increase flow, more water?"

"No, even with the rains, it could not have sped the river up. Something is pulling the water down. Something deeper than the River Hamza."

"That's not possible. There would need to be a giant drop off like a water-flow or falls over one of the Alps."

"One of the researchers who works with Hamza, the guy who discovered the river, thinks it is. He says it is entirely possible there is an enormous waterfall two miles down that then drops a portion of the Hamza another two to three miles down. All the water from these heavy rains would act as a toilet when it is flushed and pull and push anything in its path out to sea. He's the one who used that example. He had trouble with the distance though. For example, he said that the Hamza empties out underneath the ocean about two miles off shore. To have this additional underground river come out say fifty or a hundred miles out to sea, that new river would have to have dropped five or six miles under the earth's surface—maybe deeper."

"What is beneath all this causing these underground rivers?" she asked.

"The Pacific Plate."

"In the Andes, but not in Manaus, a thousand miles away from the Andes."

"They think the fish could be the canary in a mine shaft. Something pulled a living, breathing arapaima down from an underground river. Took it down much further and sucked it out into the Atlantic," Rodrigo concluded not sure that what he told the scientist made sense.

"I'm glad I did not become a rock girl. The environmental end is weird enough."

"There is another piece."

"No, no more."

"One more. Siesmic activity has increased where the Rivers Negro and Amazon meet."

"At Manaus."

"Yes, not earthquake stuff, lots of little imperceptible shakes," Rodrigo said. "So I spent some more of our precious time doing some further digging on the River Hamza. While it flows underneath the Amazon, they think where it flows under Manaus that it is at its widest—like 190 miles across."

"Not a river, an ocean."

"Really. But here's something—they have a theory that a great cavern may have formed because of the density of the jungle, year after year, over millions and millions of years, as foliage fell on top of the river. The Hamza may have been the original Amazon. All of what we know now as the Amazon jungle may have built up on top of the river."

"Is this you thinking of this or the geologists?"

"Some of both. We went out for some beers one night and played what if. But a key what if for the giant cavern theory is "what if all the rain rushing through and up into this cavern was weakening it?" Therefore, you might have some shaking or settling. Hamza, himself, did say they completed soundings down deep, and there are echoes indicating a very big space in this cavern."

"Are you saying that Manaus is sitting on top of a giant underground cavern that may be weakening."

"No, I am not. Six beers are saying that."

"Then what are you saying?"

"I think it is a lot simpler than mysterious underground rivers plunging three to six miles under the surface. I think that giant cavern beneath Manaus has filled with water from all the rain and is giving way at the bottom, creating a sinkhole that is slowly sucking everything into it, maybe even the cavern. I don't know how the arapaima gets out in the ocean, but I like my scenario better."

"I'm exhausted," she exclaimed.

"Good, let's go have a beer," Rodrigo said.

**********

# 24

*SPECIAL REPORT*

*News Brazil—All Media*

*Silvina Arancha*

*March 18, 2016*

*Manaus*

*Disaster looms for the Brazil Olympics*

*The Olympic Committee is struggling with a new challenge: three countries, as yet unidentified, have indicated they are considering a travel ban to Brazil during the Olympics for fear travelers may bring the horrific Zika virus back home with them. Two of the countries are thought to be Sierra Leone and Guinea, both of whom struggled mightily to contain the Ebola virus two years ago and both of whom have small Olympic teams.*

*Zika is a mosquito borne virus that we now have found out can be transmitted sexually. It can result in microcephaly, characterized by abnormally small heads in newborns and severe mental retardation.*

Organizers have leaked word that other actions by other countries are afoot. One European country is said to be considering a one-year quarantine on anyone travelling to and from Brazil.

Secret negotiations are also said to be underway to move some of the women's events to other countries in Europe and Asia, suggesting a two to three country Olympics. This is something that would surely rankle Brazil's President.

It is inestimable what the effects of these actions would have on Brazil. So far expenditures by the country in building out the venues to hold Olympic events and supporting infrastructure have cost the country its fortune. It is estimated that the Olympic and World Cup costs have risen to $50 billion, up from a pre-awarding estimate of $10 billion.

But the money is not the worst part. The doomsday scenario now playing out would be destructive to the national psyche. Seven years ago the mood was jubilant—Brazil's coming-out part on the world stage for a growing, prosperous nation.

Today: Economic recession, the collapse of oil prices on an oil dependent state, corruption, enormous cost overruns, delays and shoddy work on public works infrastructure projects, and the irony, the Zika virus. Brought into the country during the World Cup, it will remain long after the Olympics leave with a Brazilian medical system unable to cope with the disaster that has already infected one and a half million and resulted in over four thousand babies born with microcephaly. As Zika continues to spread, Olympic organizers are worried that fear will cause many travelers to cancel plans. With only 70 percent of tickets to Olympic events sold to date, these organizers are saying that attendance may be even lower as people stay away.

Tomorrow: If the problems above stopped here, the nation could probably cope, but: Zika is spreading more rapidly, other nations are considering travel bans to and from Brazil, female athletes may choose not to compete, and the International Olympic Committee may decide to offer other countries for women's events or for the *entire Olympics. The billions of dollars in tourism may not materialize. Especially hard hit will be the jungle city of Manaus. Hosting only six Olympic events, it was expected to draw several hundred thousand to watch the games and discover the wonders of Amazonia. Now that Manaus is ground zero for the Zika virus all bets are off.*

*Let's hope all bets are not off on Brazil's Olympic Games.*

———————————

*News Brazil—All Media*

*Silvina Arancha*

*April 4, 2016*

*Manaus*

*Olympic ticket sales tanking!*

*Ticket sales are way off for the Olympics Games. The culprit: Zika virus.*

*Along with a drop-off in ticket sales, reservations at hotels on the beaches in Rio are being cancelled at alarming rates.*

———————————

*News Brazil—All Media*

*Silvina Arancha*

*April 16, 2016*

*Manaus*

*So far there have been seventy-two confirmed Zika virus cases in the United States. Travelers contracted the virus outside of the US and brought it back in every case but one. The three leading states are Florida, sixteen; New York, twelve; and Texas, eleven.*

*New York stands out because it is such a heavily travelled to and from destination but not one where the mosquito carrying the virus would thrive.*

———————————

*News Brazil—All Media*

*Silvina Arancha*

*April 18, 2016*

*Manaus*

*Fearing the Zika virus could disrupt the Olympic Games, particularly at the remote jungle site of Manaus, Brazil has called a special conclave of the heads of the International Olympic Committee and FIFA, the sanctioning body for soccer.*

*It seems Brazil is dealing with an Olympic Committee having second thoughts on conducting six Olympic soccer matches in Manaus. The mosquito carrying the Zika virus is especially virulent in Amazonia. The Olympic Committee may find a willing partner in FIFA, which was originally against holding soccer matches so far from Rio.*

*Brazilian authorities have indicated they see no threat to participants' health if they follow proper lotion screening procedures and follow a simple rule of avoiding pregnancy until three months after they leave Brazil.*

*Good luck with that last simple rule.*

# 25

"The conversation with DeLuna will be twice as risky to have this time," said Bruno Ferreira, deputy head of the Brazilian Olympic Committee.

He was speaking with a member of the president of Brazil's administration, who was assisting him on keeping certain Olympic venues in play.

"We need him to help us again," the administrator interjected. "He may need to be stronger this time. These jerks do not understand diplomacy, only force."

"You do realize who we're dealing with here. That would be the worst thing to tell him: get tougher. There's no telling what atrocities he would commit with that guidance," then pausing said, "I will deal with him again, myself."

DeLuna and Carlos were once again summoned. DeLuna accepted the assignment once again with the guidance: "Stronger, but no deaths."

"I understand."

\*\*\*\*\*\*\*\*\*

The following day the Samuel Azevedo, the president of FIFA, soccer's governing body, received a box delivered to the long-term guest suite he had been staying at when in Rio, courtesy of the Brazilian government. The box was about a foot square and eight

165

inches deep. It was addressed to him, without a return address. He took it to his desk as his wife asked who was at the door.

"No one," he called back to her, as she was still in another room. He proceeded to open the box with a pair of scissors, slicing through the clear duct tape. A broad smile crossed his face. Stacks of $50 bills were on top. He counted one stack, a hundred bills—$5,000, twenty stacks—$100,000. This was going to be a good day he said to himself.

Beneath the money were two small boxes, like the kind a jewelry store might provide for a necklace. More gifts, maybe something for his wife, he thought. This might be an additional bonus for a favor he did the prior week. But, he thought, the bribe he received was as requested. "Oh well," he sighed.

He picked the box on the left to open first. It was light, something bounced around inside of it. He undid the plain brown wrapping paper and lifted the top off. He reeled back in horror! It was a finger. A bloody finger that appeared to be that of a girl since the finger nail was stylized in the same manner his daughter did her nails.

Then it hit him. "Eugenia! Please, God, no," he said weakly.

He placed the finger back in the box and covered it. He unwrapped the second box. He lifted the cover and found an iPhone. A note on it said, "tap here."

He did, and the phone called a number. When the phone was answered, a file began playing. A man with a mask had his arm around Eugenia's neck, holding a knife in his other hand. It was exactly as before; in fact, he thought it was the previous kidnap tape. Then the man holding his daughter spoke.

"Show Daddy your finger."

Eugenia, her face both pained and terrified held up her right hand. There was a small white bandage over her pinky finger. The man moved the knife to the other hand and pulled the bandage off revealing the bloody stump. Eugenia screamed in pain.

He gasped—it was Eugenia's finger. As he looked at her he could see the agony she was suffering.

166

"If you ever want to see this girl again, you make sure you don't fold on our previous agreement, Olympic soccer in Manaus."

"Yes, yes," was Azevedo's quick reply. "Absolutely. Please don't hurt her any more. Please take care of her hand."

"I don't care if they tell you there will be a billion mosquitos in Manaus and they will all have Zika. Soccer goes on, comprende?"

"Yes, yes."

"I know you are going to be meeting with Brazil and the Olympic Committee this afternoon. Do not give in if the Olympic Committee wants to pull out of Manaus. Do not give in."

"I will not."

"You're wondering why the money? Put the finger in your ice box. When I hear the decision to keep soccer in Manaus on the news tonight, I'll rush your daughter to Hospital Samaritano. I'll call you. You take the finger, get it to the hospital. They will reattach it. The money is to pay the doctors.

Azevedo knew he was dealing with dangerous people from the last incident. Now he knew they were mad men.

"I looked all this up. Doctors can save her finger. I snipped it just right. So you do what I told you and your daughter will go through life with ten fingers instead of nine."

"Yes, of course I will. Thank you so much. Thank you."

"One more thing" the man with the Spanish accent said. "If you don't keep this on track, if Olympic soccer is not played in Manaus, it will not be so easy to reattach your daughter's head."

Azevedo was now close to passing out from the terror and the warped mind of the monster at the other end of the conversation.

*********

"Stunned and humiliated," that's all I can say," the International Olympic Committee president said.

"Look, we said we'd come together and between the three of us, the IOC, FIFA and Brazil, we, and no one else, would decide what to do about Manaus," the president of Brazil said in the room with six people. The presidents of each sports organization and the president of Brazil, were each accompanied by a close associate.

"Juan, no one told you to go shoot your mouth off," FIFA's Azevedo was saying to his Olympic Committee counterpart.

"Listen, Azevedo, just last month you told me Manaus was out," Juan exploded. "That was the right position then, and it should be your position right now."

"Fuck," Brazil's president swore. "You two were conspiring against me," she said, pounding the table separating them.

"You're damn right we were. You wouldn't listen," Juan continued, exasperated. "All you cared about was filling the venues to capture some of your misspent fortune."

"Asshole," she stood up. "You're the one who said make this first class. Make Brazil first class. I bought into your hype."

Juan did not like the put-down, and by a woman in a man's culture. "And who's worried about the athletes, their health? The Zika virus is serious. You're not doing enough, and you," he turned to face his FIFA counterpart, "when did you start drinking from her water fountain? If we take Manaus off the table, everyone is happy. No athletes have to go into the jungle. And for what? Six fucking games. It's ludicrous."

Azevedo pushed his chair back from the round table. "As usual you're wrong Juan. Manaus is a sensitive decision. It's why I was open minded about it. I was against it, for it, against it and for it. In each of those cases I listened."

He was cut off by the IOC president. Juan screamed, "Yes, you listened to the highest bidder. Who's paying you this time," and he looked at the president of Brazil. He was about to say it, but catching her glare, he demurred.

"I'm satisfied it is not only safe but because of the redoubling of efforts to eradicate Zika by madam president, it might be the safest of all the venues."

The president of Brazil looked at the president of FIFA and could have kissed him at that moment. But only that moment, otherwise she despised the weasel and his corruptness. She was aware of what had happened to his daughter Eugenia, the prior year. She was also aware of the package he received earlier in the day and that Eugenia is currently missing a finger. Nonetheless, she was grateful.

Under the rules of their agreement, they decided that a majority of the three would constitute a final decision. Although, ever thorough, if they sided against her, she would have had them both arrested for bribery and corruption. She had film of both of them accepting brides, filmed at the suites provided by Brazil.

That night, News Brazil stated they had learned that all three parties agreed that the games would go forward in Manaus as planned. They were satisfied with the extensive spraying taking place that would make it among the safest of all Olympic venues.

Eugenia's finger was reattached in a late night emergency operation.

# 26

*News Brazil—All Media*

*Silvina Arancha*

*July 25, 2016*

*Manaus*

*Breaking news! Zika virus holding down attendance at Olympics*

*With a little more than a week to go before the opening ceremonies for the Olympic Games ticket sales are lagging and venues are expected to be full to only 80 percent of capacity.*

*Olympic officers worry there will be thousands of empty seats at premier Olympic events, even including the opening ceremonies in Rio.*

*What we are hearing: Government orders—fill the stadiums. Unsold tickets by this weekend will be given away so that every event will by full to overflowing.*

## July 31, 2016

Chunk DeLuna, hosting the second large party in a month at his home, was about to become an admired, respectable man, when Puckerlips, the parrot, spoke from across the large marble salon filled with revelers. "Pretty bird," the parrot said, cackling the words Lupe Monserrat taught him when she posed him for his portrait. The portrait no longer hung in the center of the room having been slashed and destroyed by a jealous DeLuna. It had been replaced by an earlier and smaller version of Puckerlips, a model for the final, that the bird was now admiring.

The Brazilian senator from the state of Bahia stepped forward in the center of the room beneath the painting. The room went silent as the senator took a breath to speak. "Pretty bird," the parrot intoned to uproarious laughter.

"Yes, yes, pretty bird," the senator said to more laughter. One of the DeLuna housemen at the rear of the room reached up and pulled the cover over Puckerlips' large cage after getting an eye from DeLuna.

"As I was about to say, before my friend admired his painting," the senator said to further laughter, "our gracious host, Mr. Juan DeLuna is making all Brazilians proud with the beautiful Olympic Stadium he has built in Manaus."

DeLuna, for one of the few times in his life blushed, and his eyes looked downward for a moment. There was loud applause for the man for whom all gathered owed their livelihood or their enhanced livelihood.

The Senator continued, "In five days the opening ceremonies will take place in Rio, followed two days later by the initial soccer matches in Manaus. All of us, as you know, and I hope you appreciate the significance, will be guests of Mr. DeLuna at the new stadium.

Mr. DeLuna, we are all truly grateful and honored to represent our state and Brazil when we travel to Manaus."

The hundred or so guests erupted in applause and the senator stood aside beckoning DeLuna to speak.

"Obrigada, Senator," DeLuna said as he stepped forward and beside the senator who shook his hand enthusiastically. "And thank you all for coming and for your support for CDL Enterprisa in this most serious undertaking."

"A great man," said the procurement director from the state of Amazonia to others next to him but no one in particular. Two congressional representatives nodded enthusiastically, one saying to the other, "He should be in politics; he knows how to get things done." They had successfully sponsored a bill moving certain historical landmarks in Manaus to make way for the Stadium so that the overall site would also encompass a five-acre plot owned by DeLuna. These guests owed their new wealth to the bribes DeLuna paid them or the debts he released them from.

DeLuna smiled, his gold canine teeth gleaming in the light, those teeth always the reminder of the beast that lurked.

"And," DeLuna said, puffing up his wide chest, "before we fly to Manaus on our charter flight next week, I have one more surprise. When you fly from Recife to Manaus, you are taking a small diversion south," he paused looking at the anticipation on the faces, and now shouted, "to the opening ceremonies in Rio." The guests had questions on their faces; they began looking at each other, not quite sure what DeLuna was saying. "I have arranged everything. You have great seats four rows from the president of our country." DeLuna looked at the questions on their faces. These people, these friends, these paid-off bureaucrats were all from similar backgrounds—from poor families, part of the new middle class being established. They worked hard, did their jobs, and as is the custom throughout the country, those with influence sold it for the extra income.

"You're going to the grand opening of the Olympics. CDL has contacted all of your employers and bosses and got permission for you to have the extended time off for the work you have done supporting this great effort," and now he saw the affect. Tears were flowing from the eyes of many; smiles pushed forth at same time. It was only occasionally that recognition was given for individual effort, criminal or otherwise. A few of the younger men in the middle of the room began jumping up and down, yelling, "Viva Brazil, viva Brazil." Three women on the left side of the room began dancing, holding hands as they went around in a circle. They were the highest earning prostitutes from DeLuna's brothels in Manaus, taking care of his union workers building the stadium. Bedlam began erupting as the entire gathering realized what DeLuna was telling them, what he was doing for them. Silent pledges of allegiance to this generous man were being recited in the hearts of many.

Chunk DeLuna was pleased. Everyone was happy.

# 27

The preliminary game had scarcely begun. The heat of the afternoon made it a steaming concrete jungle on the edge of the steaming Amazon jungle. The first crack appeared on the wall at the top of the stadium, which on this day was full to its capacity of fifty-two thousand fans. In section 17, row 88, seats A16 and A18 sat two fans, two teenaged boys who plunged into the abyss that opened beneath them. The wall shuttered as the ground beneath it gave way. As the stadium curved at its southeast corner, it began melting away. Section after section collapsed as a giant sink hole opened its hideous mouth, wider and wider.

Patrons in the northwest corner stared in disbelief as the opposite end of the stadium disappeared. Panic set in as they watched row after row drop and they watched the flailing hands as the bottom of this sports site drop from beneath the fans opposite them.

Four hundred sixty people died, an estimated 230 were missing, and another 2,200 were hospitalized. The nearest local hospital had 150 beds when the injured started arriving; then the hospital expanded, first to the stadium's parking lot, then to the local high school and its soccer field.

Police, fire fighters, fans of the game, local citizens were all pressed into service. It took more than forty-eight hours to extract all of the injured and non-injured from the great sinkhole that swallowed up the southeast corner, just to the right of the goal. On this opening day of Brazil's Olympics soccer venue in Manaus, the goal had no shots on it.

People could be heard screaming in agony and fear. The injured and scared cried from the black hole. After several hours of utter chaos, a system began to emerge. Ropes and ladders had been secured; triage areas opened; doctors, nurses and EMTs located. An army unit, responsible for security in this area of the state, was stationed on the outskirts of the city. Soldiers were called to duty and with several large trucks began assisting ambulances in shuttling the injured from the battlefield that was Manaus Stadium to other hospitals further away when more intensive care was required.

It was the army unit's commander who described the scene as a battlefield. "I was with the UN in Kosovo, and I never saw anything this bad. It was worse than any human destruction we saw in that war zone," the shaken leader explained.

Over the next several days, the depth of the tragedy began to spread across Brazil and the soccer loving world. A brand new stadium was undermined, it was theorized, by an underground river beneath the Amazon River, a twin called the River Hamza.

In Brasilia, the nation's capital, pride at winning the right to host the Olympics soared for the first two years after the announcement in 2009, then reality set it. The costs were sinking the economy. The infrastructure costs to put on the Olympics were grossly underestimated. Running the Olympics was to be a profitable event, to the tune of billions of dollars in TV and attendance fees, along with billions more in tourism during and immediately after the events. Then more billions were to follow as the world would have the opportunity to see this burgeoning giant in the jungle with fabulous people, stunning seasides like Rio and Recife and the great Amazon jungle. But the infrastructure—buildings to house the competitors, the arenas and stadiums, and the support structure to house and transport the millions that were expected—had not been properly planned and financed. The scale and speed required to host the games seemed doable. That was the word the president used, "doable," repeatedly. If she said it was doable, even if it wasn't, it was. Optimism, the sin of the hopeful, overrode judgement.

Common sense was in short supply when assessing the nation's capabilities; greed, however, was abundant. Many sitting national legislators were getting their share. Before the Olympics it was already bad enough that three hundred of Brazil's eight hundred national legislators had been convicted of serious crimes and were still in their positions.

Yet, the president, with sheer will power persuaded, calmed, and led the nation through its doubt. She reinforced the future destiny that was about to be the new Brazil. They believed her.

**********

"Fuck," the president screamed. "Of course they believed me. I'm the president. I said we would host the most successful games in Olympic history. And on the first day, the fucking first day in Manaus, we have a tragedy." She slammed her hand down on the table. "I want answers—how could this have happened."

In front of the flaming president were assembled two senators, three cabinet ministers, the head of Brazil's Olympic committee, and the project director for the Olympics. There was a shiver that ran through the middle-aged men, each in a suit. They had all been in attendance, the day earlier, at different Olympic events.

"FuuucccccKKK!" she raged. "Tell me, who is responsible for this?" she screamed while looking daggers at the project director. He became afraid. He thought, a woman could do this to me, never. "TELL ME," she shrieked at the top of her lungs. The project director looked at her. She came out from behind her desk. She was as tall as him. The president grabbed the director by his lapels and yanked him to within inches of her face. "TELL ME YOU MISERABLE BASTARD. HOW DID THIS HAPPEN?"

A tear came to his right eye, then the left. They rolled down his cheeks.

"You're crying. You fuck. We have hundreds of people dead because of your incompetence and you're crying?" She paced back and forth for a moment, trying to get a grip on this crisis. "You get the fuck out of my office and come back here in two hours. TWO

FUCKING HOURS! And tell me what went wrong. Who fucked this up."

He stood looking at her. The tears flowed freely.

"GET THE FUCK OUT," she said, then turning to the head of the Olympic committee, she screamed. "Get him the fuck out of my sight. All of you get the fuck out of my sight."

\*\*\*\*\*\*\*\*\*\*

In two hours they did not have answers. In the coming days, in the bowels of the building where the Olympics were planned, the officers and legislators responsible gathered. They began reviewing the Manaus stadium from conception, through the fights that said Brazil did not need a fifty-two thousand seat stadium in the jungle. They examined the notes on the political battles that followed, the approvals, the architect's renderings, the approved designs, and the contracting process and the awards. They pulled out project plan documents for every stage of the stadium, budgets, costs, deadlines and the surveys for the site.

CDL Enterprisa, general contractor for Manaus Stadium was about to be called to task.

And when the chief civil engineer called CDL Enterprisa three days after the collapse of the stadium, Chunk DeLuna was among the missing.

Oh, he had been there, that is, at the stadium. He beamed with pride as he and his party had prime seats for the opening game at the stadium. He bragged and preened as he showed his guests what he and CDL had built. Then it was all gone.

DeLuna's party had been sitting midfield looking right at the goal as a midfielder broke free and raced towards the goal. The Kenyan dodged two Chileans as they tried to assist the goal keeper. The Kenyan kicked the ball, and it went high over the goal. From where DeLuna sat, it looked like the ball knocked the southeast end of the stadium down. Up went the ball, down came the stadium wall—slowly. That was how DeLuna saw it, like slow motion. First a couple of rows, then it all began falling from the top down. Then it became like a star burst, arms began flailing. People fled in every direction away from the hole that was opening up in Chunk DeLuna's stadium.

Chunk's mouth was open. That southeast corner of his beautiful stadium was dropping into the ground. DeLuna could not get his mind around where the stadium was falling to. After several minutes of shock at what had occurred and watching as people began moving back towards the great tragedy that had occurred, DeLuna ushered the eleven friends in his party out of the stadium.

# 28

Chunk DeLuna's head was pounding as he woke from a restless sleep. His troubles sprang forth overwhelming sleep; his mind was instantly cleared of early morning fog. One by one the challenges appeared: yesterday's stadium collapse was first in line followed by issues with one Olympic village building that had major water damage due to faulty plumbing, and finally, a myriad of lower level issues like a government minister who was rolling over in a federal inquiry into suspected bribes paid by DeLuna's CDL Enterprisa.

Chunk bounded out of bed and started doing push-ups. After one set of one hundred, the pressure on his brain abated somewhat only to make room for the dilemma of Lupe and her painter. He quickly changed into running shorts, tank-top t-shirt and sneakers and bolted out the front door. He was mindful that this day he may be arrested as TV stations nation-wide were calling for the heads of the people who built the doomed Amazonia stadium.

He thought about Lupe as he ran. He had never seen her the way she looked as they left the stadium. She kept asking him, "How could this have happened?" Over and over. Nothing else, just that. Was it an accusation? Was she just dumb struck? He did not ask her, but when she asked to stay at the Intercontinental Hotel on the Boa Viagem, alone, he knew. She blamed him. She did not want to return to their home. She did not say it, but he knew her thought: "You took all the credit, now take all the blame." That was the smug

179

way she talked to him about some of his shadier deals that didn't work out. Maybe he did need to take the blame for this, maybe not.

The conniver in DeLuna had started thinking. The problem was not with the stadium. It was underneath it. The people who did the soil samples and the surveyors and the engineers who instructed CDL on the foundation, they should all be blamed. They should have found what was now known: where the Rio Negro meets the Amazon at Manaus, in that same enormous river basin, also flows the world's largest underground river, the River Hamza, only discovered in 2011.

On the news that DeLuna watched before he left his home, geologists were speculating that a river flowing underneath the stadium was a branch of the underground River Hamza and that branch of the river flowed through an enormous cavern. Spring rains were so heavy the cavern filled and the water reached the dome, eroding it, turning it to mush at the same time creating a sinkhole at the bottom of the cavern. The great weight of the stadium sitting directly above the dome caused parts of it to collapse into the cavern and then further into the sinkhole at the bottom of the cavern. The last part explained why so many of the missing were presumed dead. The collapse of the cavern sucked them into the sinkhole, deeper into the earth.

To DeLuna this spelt opportunity. What was his lawyer always telling him: plausible deniability. "How could we possibly have known an underground river flowed under the stadium since it was not discovered an underground river even existed until a year after we began construction."

The news showed rescued soccer fans being pulled from the gaping hole that was once part of the stadium. Their clothes were soaked; they were wet and freezing. Reporters early to the scene the prior day began interviewing them.

"We just fell, straight down," began one male fan, about twenty-five years old, "like someone pulled the floor from beneath us."

The reporter, live on air, moved his mic to another rescued fan, "We hit water. People all around were splashing. Blackness everywhere but we could see light above." The fan sneezed and caught his breath, "We were drowning. The water was carrying us away. Some of us were close to dirt and we swam to the side. It was like a river bank. I think it was a river we were in."

That was the image DeLuna kept seeing as he thought about what to do now. He had arrived back in Recife in the company jet, on the three-hour flight from Manaus at 4 a.m. He dropped Lupe off at the Intercontinental, and when he arrived home, part of that same report was being broadcast. It aired many times into the early morning. Chunk placed himself in front of the TV watching the horror of what he had created, until he fell asleep.

The news stations in Recife had been covering the event all night. After all it was a tragedy of major proportions: the national sport, the opening game of the Olympics in Manaus, the miraculous transformation of Brazil from third world to first world, and the eyes of the world on beautiful Brazil.

That was it then, DeLuna reasoned in his primitive but highly alert brain. No construction could withstand faulty soil samples, of not knowing a river existed beneath the proposed stadium, of a sinking site that a stadium with 350,000 tons of cement and steel would sit on, and of poor advice from the French engineers, who were originally engaged to assess the site. He would go on the offensive. He would join the outrage. "My stadium, my fans, my Brazil. Hang the bastards that did this to us!"

DeLuna smiled as he now ran along the beach, scheming with each stride. He was so focused that for the first time ever he did not stop to look at girls on the beach. He pulled his cell phone out of the small pouch on his right side, ran his finger over the screen to his lawyer's name and tapped it.

"Miglio, this is Chunk," Miglio knew, "I know. Good morning, boss."

"It's not good, you idiot, but it's going to get better," DeLuna snarled, "You saw the news?"

"Yes, tragic. Is that us?"

"That is our stadium. And we are outraged over what has happened. I want you to set up a press conference."

During the course of a wide-ranging interview at the stadium site in Manaus the following day, DeLuna played the deeply distraught mourner over the loss of life, highly humiliated for Brazil, and personally enraged over the incompetence of surveyors and engineers who did the initial work that missed the underground river, leaving "my stadium to fall into the abyss." DeLuna began to cry.

DeLuna even arranged for one of his engineers to explain with a chart where the fault lay. On the left hand side of the chart, divided by a black line, were the names of the companies who had responsibility to understand the soil conditions, underground issues and foundation structural requirements. On the right hand side was CDL Enterprisa. "The bastards on the left told us how to build it, what to build it on and we did." DeLuna then stood in front of the CDL part and pointed at each of the three engineering companies "These thieves let you down. They murdered our fellow citizens with their incompetence, and they shamed Brazil in front of the world." For emphasis, when a reporter asked a question afterwards, DeLuna said he "would testify under oath against these killers to ensure that justice is served."

**********

The president of Brazil viewed a replay of DeLuna's press conference. She liked his approach. She adopted it. Brazil is horrified. The French let us down. But even then, could any of us have foreseen something like the massive spring rains swelling the branch of the great underground river. This river that undermined the stadium site was barely known to exist. Sympathy and admiration for Brazil was occurring around the world. Poor Brazil, bravely carrying on. The president was being lauded for her leadership in the face of disaster. Over the course of the next three days, the Olympics continued and the clamor began to die down since it was now appearing no one was at fault—it was an act of God.

# 29

On the ninth day after the Manaus Stadium collapse, Joao Silva, the surveyor fired from the Manaus project called *Dario Do Amazonas,* one of the major newspapers of Manaus. After a brief discussion by phone and a first meeting with Silvina Arancha, the reporter who spoke with him, Silvina sensed a larger story and asked if they could do a joint interview with *News Brazil—All Media—TV,* the Manaus TV station, which also owned the newspaper. This would ensure more national coverage and Silvina would get to write the print version for *News Brazil—All Media.* Silva agreed, and they met the next day at the offices of *News Brazil TV.*

That evening the interview was broadcast in Manaus at the dinner hour and picked up by all Brazilian TV outlets for the late evening news. The next morning the front page of the *Diario do Amazonas* carried the full interview with a headline that screamed, "They knew the Stadium was sinking!" Silvina's print version of the story also appeared in all major newspapers around the world through *News Brazil—All Media.*

In the TV interview, a man and a woman were sitting across from each other separated by a small table that had water glasses on it. The woman was immediately recognizable in Manaus as Michelle Montes, a former beauty queen turned TV news anchor. The camera's eye, as had become common, was at waist level and showcased Michelle's legs to a level above the thigh. Joao Silva, who sat across from her, was dressed in a beige linen shirt and brown slacks and looked nervous.

*Interviewer: Good evening, my name is Michelle Montes and tonight I have an exclusive interview with Joao Silva who has told me a remarkable story of malfeasance at the collapsed Olympic Stadium here in Manaus. Thank you for coming forward, Mr. Silva.*

*The camera zoomed in on Silva, who nodded as he began sweating under the stage lighting of the newsroom set.*

"Mr. Silva, please tell our audience your name and occupation."

*Silva: I am Joao Silva, and I am a surveyor.*

*Montes: How long have you been a surveyor, Mr. Silva?*

*Silva: Nineteen years.*

*Montes: What are you working on now?*

*Silva: Nothing. I am unemployed.*

*Montes: How did you come to be unemployed?*

*Silva: I was fired as the surveyor on the Manaus Olympic Stadium site.*

*Montes: This is the same Olympic Stadium that collapsed last week?*

*Silva: Yes.*

*Montes: Why were you fired?*

*Silva: I found that the ground under the project site was sinking.*

*Montes: Wait! This was before the collapse of the stadium?*

*Silva: Yes.*

*Montes: You're are telling us that you and others knew the stadium was sinking before it collapsed?*

*Silva: Yes.*

*Montes: (Here the camera zoomed in on Montes and showed both her anguish and puzzlement as she pressed Silva.) Why didn't you say something?*

*Silva: (Who was now sweating profusely with drops running from his forehead to his cheeks. His linen shirt was soaked on his upper chest. He reached for a tissue from the box on the table and mopped his brow.) I did.*

*Montes: Who did you tell?*

*Silva: We had taken a final survey before pouring the walls and the seating section for the stadium.*

*Montes: (She interrupted, demanding.) Why is this important?*

*Silva: We do a six-point survey on the area when we first start out on a project. Then before the major segments of any project are poured to ensure absolute uniformity of something as large as a stadium, we re-survey. We re-take those same six points to be absolutely certain they match.*

*Montes: OK, and did they match?*

*Silva: No.*

*Montes: No. Were they a little off?*

*Silva: No.*

*Montes: (The drama queen was now in her element.) What do you mean "no?" I thought you told me they were off?*

*Silva: You asked if they were off a little. The answer is no. They were off a lot.*

*Montes: A lot? How much is a lot?*

*Silva: One meter on four points.*

*Montes: (Following their previously discussed approach to the interview, Montes would ask all the questions and add the emotion. His role was to be professional, matter of fact and therefore believable.) One meter, that doesn't seem like a lot to me.*

*Silva: (He leaned in here.) That is a gigantic amount to be off!*

*Montes: How was it off? How would you describe what was happening?*

*Silva: The ground was sinking! In the two years from the start in 2010 where we took the first reading to where we were on the final readings in 2012, the ground sank by a meter. Never before have I seen anything like this, not even a millimeter. I re-checked every point three times, recalibrated my instruments. Still—one meter.*

At this point in the interview, Carlos who had been watching it called Chunk DeLuna

"Do you have you TV on?" he asked his boss.

*Montes: And what did you do when you saw your readings were off? (The camera, which had been zoomed in on Montes, panned slowly, increasing the drama, over to Silva.)*

*Silva: I told the project engineer.*

*Montes: And what happened? Tell us … (she said impatiently, heightening the moment).*

*Silva: What happened? What happened is I got fired.*

*Montes: Just like that? The readings were off and you got fired?*

*Silva: (Now feeling belittled, he pushed back.) No, not just like that! It was the day they were to begin pouring the stadium walls. One week before, I had taken the readings. They were off, and I told the project engineer. On the day we were to begin the pour, the project engineer told me the project manager wanted me to resurvey. The readings were the same. The ground had sunk one meter in two years. After I gave the project engineer the second set of readings, he asked me to recalibrate my instruments. I had. Nothing changed. Then he told me to go to lunch. After a couple of hours, he came back and fired me.*

*Montes: What did he say.*

*Silva: He said my work on the project was completed. He would not need me anymore.*

*Montes: Was your work complete?*

*Silva: It could have been. But there was plenty of continuing survey work through 2013, 14 and 15 that needed to be done as the various stages of the site were completed. Especially since the site had sunk and to figure out how to rectify it.*

*Montes: Weren't you hired to do that?*

*Silva: I was the project surveyor. The project surveyor stays on the project until it is complete. If you check you will see that there was a new project surveyor hired after I was let go.*

*Montes: Let me summarize. What you have told us is that the ground beneath the Manaus Olympic Stadium had sunk one meter in the two years since the project began. Is that correct? In 2012 the site was a meter lower than in 2010?*

*Silva: Yes.*

*Montes: And once you told your boss on the project that the ground was sinking, you were fired."*

*Silva: Yes.*

Fifteen minutes after the broadcast, the Olympic Project Director was on the phone with the president of Brazil.

"Madam President, did you see the news."

"Yes, I just saw the video clip," the President answered.

"We had no knowledge of this," the Olympic Project Director said with fear in his voice.

"I don't believe you!" she screamed into the phone.

"I'll resign if you wish."

"No you won't! You'll be in my office tomorrow morning at 7 a.m. with exactly what happened: what sequence, who knew and what they did or did not do about it. It seems like the surveyor was the only one who knew what he was doing," she concluded.

"Yes, ma'am."

\*\*\*\*\*\*\*\*\*\*

The president, exhausted from the rollercoaster of the past ten days, collapsed in her chair. She felt as if she were falling into that giant sinkhole in the jungle. Just when she thought she had escaped, it was sucking her in.

# PART

# 5

# 30

DeLuna's world of violence had left him a growing, unbalanced ledger of hate. It was a ledger that could only be balanced by revenge. The only question was: who would act? Hate of Chunk for beheading the sister of a Salvadoran drug dealer, hate of DeLuna for killing a Senator's daughter in a vat of acid. Hate of DeLuna by the families of deposed and murdered DeLuna cement executives. Hate of DeLuna from Estephan for his treatment of Lupe. Hate of DeLuna by the President of Brazil for destroying her defining moment on the world stage.

In all this time, the criminal enterprise CDL flourished, partly because of DeLuna's maniacal drive for control, but mostly because of the confident demeanor of Carlos and the loyalty of his original underlings, Pedro, Paco and Raphael. It was Carlos who balanced DeLuna's volatility with calm in a crisis. Chunk was smart enough to realize the gifts that Carlos possessed were not in his own makeup. It was why Carlos ran the cement business and made it profitable, it was why he was the number two man in the organization, and it was why DeLuna relied on him for advice. Advice that increasingly, as CDL became more far flung and complex, Carlos realized was necessary. In fact, it had become Carlos who was making decisions, running the business. DeLuna was moving to an emeritus position in the enterprise, mainly because complexity was confounding him, and Federal prosecutors were out to imprison him. It was a tightrope that Carlos walked, always letting Chunk know which decision he made but not seeking approval beforehand.

And so, when Chunk came to Carlos with the problem of Lupe and Estephan, Carlos gave advice as confidently as he did in other business matters. This was a mistake.

"Chunk, what do you expect?"

"Loyalty, love. I give her everything. I took her from the slum," DeLuna confided, running a hand through his thick black hair. "Christ, he's old enough to be her father, her grandfather. You've seen the guy at Lupe's art show, right?"

"Yes, Chunk," Carlos said, still in a listening mode, still taking in the heat as the wounded beast railed on.

"And when I asked her, I knew, I fucking knew, but when I asked her what was going on, know what she said?"

"Yes, you told me."

"Fucking right I told you. She said I was crazy. I accuse her of being with Estephan and she says to me, "Chunk, he's old enough to be my father." How's that for telling me to fuck off," the bull continued his rage, now rising from his chair and pacing. It was when Chunk paced that Carlos got nervous. It usually meant that the magma underneath was superheating and that an eruption was imminent.

"Chunk, you broke her arm."

"I broke her arm because she wouldn't tell the truth," DeLuna growled, his face contorted as he gripped the air with both hands and broke Lupe's arm again in his mind. "Fucking bitch."

"This isn't going to end well."

"What are you talking about," DeLuna snapped at Carlos.

"You've got to be careful. If Lupe changes her story while she's in the hospital, we could be in trouble."

"Any more trouble than I already am?" DeLuna ranted. "She won't. She fell down the stairs. That's it. If she changes her story, she will fall down the stairs. She'll fall off a building."

"Those bruises on her face, the black eyes. It looks worse."

"She won't. What the fuck is wrong with you. Bitch'll be back in line."

Here is where Carlos made his mistake.

"I don't think you know Lupe as well as you think you do," Carlos said.

DeLuna stopped whatever interactive thought process was happening in his mind. His brain went blank. He turned, now squarely facing Carlos directly. "What did you just say?" DeLuna asked, flatly, coldly.

Carlos saw a different DeLuna also but decided his friend needed some coaching. "Chunk, she's not the same sixteen-year-old girl who came out of the projects. Look at her. She's a beautiful woman. She's growing. She's discovering herself."

DeLuna's muscles were tightening under the snug fitting linen shirt. His powerful arms were pulsing, like a boxer stepping in the ring, anticipating action. The shirt was getting tighter on his body. Carlos could sense the tension building. He needed to help Chunk through this.

"Chunk, you still treat her like she's a child. Beating the shit out of her when you …"

Carlos paused, now looking at Chunk whose left eye began to twitch, blink, like it was sending a coded message. DeLuna began calmly, "Tell me what you mean," he said not betraying his inner rage.

"You fucking destroyed her painting of the bird. She loved that thing."

"That thing insulted me. She was saying things to that bird that were disloyal," DeLuna said, barely able to squeeze the words out of his clamped jaw. "And the bird repeated them."

"And you couldn't talk with her about that?"

"No."

"This isn't about the painting or the bird. It's about Estephan."

"It's about Estephan," DeLuna repeated in a singsong children's manner, mocking Carlos.

"She was more proud of that painting than anything she had done in her life."

"It was a fucking painting of a bird."

"No, Chunk, it was something more. She accomplished it."

"Who says so."

"Estephan."

"Estephan?" DeLuna said warily. "Estephan wants to fuck her, of course he'd tell her the painting is an accomplishment."

"Chunk. Think. Even you liked it, before you didn't like it. You said yourself you were proud of what she was doing, improving herself. You were going to get her space to show her work."

"I was wrong," DeLuna concluded and then doubled back, "How the fuck do you know Estephan thought it was good."

"Lupe told me," Carlos said, realizing that he was treading into the fringes of jealously that dominated DeLuna's behavior when it came to Lupe.

"Chunk, I'm going to tell you this for your own good," Carlos said, summoning up the courage that he knew would cost him. "You're losing Lupe. She's growing—you have to give her room and support her."

DeLuna's head was now hurting. At the top, on the right and left sides the pressure was painful. His teeth were clenched so tight Carlos could hear the grinding as he moved his jaw from left to right. His knuckles were poking through the white skin of his hands as he rubbed them against each other.

Just for a second Carlos saw these things. He had seen Chunk boiling before. This was different. The pressure cooker was starting to vibrate. The little man was about to explode. The volcano that lingered beneath the surface had a molten core; it was pushing the lava up to the surface. Containment was about to end.

"How do you know these things about my girl? How?" DeLuna screamed as he leaped onto Carlos.

Later when the beating had ended, when Carlos lay bleeding in a heap on the expensive carpet of DeLuna's sun room that overlooked the Atlantic on a perfect day, DeLuna thought to himself that Lupe would be upset. She had just bought that carpet.

# 31

"Lupeeeee!" the parrot screeched. It was if the bird knew.

Chunk DeLuna reached in his cage as Puckerlips jumped to a corner. Chunk moved his short powerful arm in further, almost able to grab the parrot. Puckerlips took his beak and drove it down into Chunk's hand, in the soft tissue between his thumb and forefinger. "Aggghhhh!" Chunk yelled as blood came pouring out of the gash.

The cage hung from a hook that was attached to a six-foot-high floor stand that arched over to the part where the hook held the cage. Chunk grabbed the cage and tipped it over, sending the stand and the cage crashing onto the mosaic tile floor.

The bird had pulled its feathers tight against its body and rolled over as the cage hit the floor. Puckerlips hopped up as DeLuna leaned over the cage, sticking his hand in again trying to reach the elusive avian creature from Amazonia. The bird hopped to one side, then the other, no longer speaking but making noises in his throat. The bird could not process what was happening.

Chunk grew furious that he could not reach the bird. "I'm going to get you, you little bastard."

"Asshole!" Puckerlips barked at DeLuna, infuriating him more. DeLuna jumped on the cage attempting to crush it with his weight. The steel cage did not collapse. The bird tried to make it to the exit hole but DeLuna's hand got there first and grabbed him. The bird again drove its beak into the back of DeLuna's hand, opening another wound and forcing his grip to yield.

DeLuna picked up the cage, pulled it off the hook that it was still attached to even in its fallen state. Sensing doom, the bird let out a long howl, a sound that would come from a dog rather than a parrot.

When DeLuna, pulling the cage behind him, got to the French doors that led to the patio, he turned to the bird and said, "We're going for a little swim."

Right then Puckerlips hopped up and bit one of DeLuna's fingers holding the cage. The bird kept a powerful grip on the bone of the first finger of Chunk's left hand. DeLuna took his right hand, already bloodied, and smashed it against the cage trying to frighten the bird into letting go.

It did not work. The bird had locked on and was not releasing Chunk's finger that was clenched along with his others between the spaces of the cage's bars.

"You think you're tough," DeLuna said to the bird. "We'll see who let's go first," Chunk continued as he dragged the cage to the edge of the pool. "Hold your nose," he laughed and swung the cage over the water as he jumped into the end of the pool that was eight feet deep. Bird, cage and DeLuna disappeared beneath the surface.

Seconds passed. The water grew red from DeLuna's blood that was oozing out from three wounds to his hands. It was a battle of wills between two bird brains. Never before had a bird fought for its life so bravely. Never before had a man stooped to such incompetence or had a man been so outsmarted by a bird.

DeLuna's plan was to reach into the cage, take the bird in hand and suffocate it. He would then place it back in the cage and let Lupe discover Puckerlips dead when she returned from her painting lesson.

More seconds passed. Suddenly DeLuna's head surfaced, and a moment later he swung the cage up out of the water onto the pool's edge. A drenched, skinny, pathetic looking creature emerged still clamped onto DeLuna's finger. It knew letting go of his stumpy digit meant death. Then just as fiercely as he fought, Puckerlips released the finger and fell over, dead, onto the floor of the cage.

Chunk, his finger a bloodied mess pulled it gingerly from the bar of the metal cage. The skin remained on the bar. Puckerlips had ripped the skin off. Blood was now everywhere, gushing from torn veins in the finger. A small muscle from the finger flopped limply, torn from an attached tendon.

"Fuck, fuck!" DeLuna screamed both from the pain and damage the bird had done to his hands. DeLuna was also feeling fear at how extensively the bird had gouged his hands. He would need to get to a hospital quickly. It was his luck that no one was in the house. It was his bad luck that he had planned the murder of Puckerlips that way. To get rid of the bird, to stop the insults and to get Lupe's attention, Chunk had carefully planned the murder of the bird.

It would need to be a day Lupe would be at her painting lesson.

"Bye, Lupe," Puckerlips said in response to her saying, "Bye, Puckerlips," and she was out the door.

It was also the maid's day off, and Chunk had sent the gardener to the nursery to buy a plant.

Puckerlips sensed danger early on, when the house was empty but for he and Chunk. The bird paced nervously, hopping back and forth across the center perch in the cage. The door to the cage was always left open and Puckerlips had free rein to roam where he wanted in the house.

This day he stayed close to home; he did not venture out of the cage.

Chunk passed the cage several times, looking in at the bird.

"Today's the day, asshole," DeLuna said, using the birds favorite greeting for him.

"Asshole," the bird repeated.

Chunk slammed the outside of the cage. He put his face up against the cage and growled. The bird lunged at DeLuna, its beak protruding from the cage and barely missing DeLuna as he retreated.

The taunting continued by both parties. DeLuna came by a short time later and laughed at the bird, saying, "Lupe's gonna miss her little birdie," sticking his finger between the bars as the bird nipped him. Chunk pulled his finger back as the pain set in.

"Fuck you, Chunk," the bird yelled. "Fuck you, asshole," he went on with the same accent as Lupe, who had taught Puckerlips these expressions after beatings by Chunk.

Now with the deed done, the taking of the life of Lupe's baby, another murder committed, DeLuna searched for gauze to wrap his finger. He needed to see a doctor. This was a serious wound that needed attention, he rationalized, or he might lose the finger.

This was not good. His plan had totally failed. Suffocating the bird would have seemed like a more natural death. Lupe would still accuse him, but only he would know for sure. He would buy her a replacement bird, but one that was mute.

DeLuna just could not pull off a simple murder. He always made a mess; whether it was an acid bath for a Senator's daughter, a hail of bullets for the enemy, or a decapitation to keep a competitor quiet, he always made a mess of things.

The gardener came in the house.

Relieved, DeLuna said, "I need help, Jose."

Jose on seeing the mess, the blood everywhere on DeLuna, on the floor, in the pool, the bird's cage out in the pool area, said "What happened, boss," and then spying the bird at the bottom of the cage added, "Is that Puckerlips?"

"Yes," DeLuna moaned.

"What the hell happened?" the gardener asked.

# 32

"Araghh," DeLuna moaned as he sat up on the floor. Soaked in blood, a chill ran through his body. He was not dead. It had been a nightmare. He had been looking down at himself in a pool of blood. Not knowing who had killed him but knowing it could have been any of scores of people. And Carlos, knowing! Carlos knew who killed him. But why didn't DeLuna know who had killed him.

The nightmare was starting to fade as all dreams do back into the unconscious. But DeLuna would not forget this dream. It was horrible, like the one the week before when he killed the parrott, Puckerlips. He dreamt the bird had almost severed his finger and he drowned it. Well, for that, and for swearing at him all the time. Then DeLuna looked at his bandaged hand; his finger had been almost severed. It was not a dream—he had killed the bird. But why were his hand and chest covered in blood? Why was there blood on the floor?

He was having trouble; his mind was under so much pressure he could not tell reality from a dream. He never had nightmares like this before. Not before the collapse of the stadium—then a series of dreams of young boys screaming for help as they hung onto the collapsing stadium, then watching them fall. Not into water but into fire. Were they falling into hell? He wondered for the first time was that him hanging on, was that him falling into the fires of hell? The dreams were getting worse, and he was having more trouble sleeping.

Was it Wednesday? He did not bound out of bed. It was a struggle; he longed for more sleep, a restful sleep. A day at the beach would be helpful. He could nap there on the sand. Only he was not sleeping, he was not dreaming. DeLuna was covered in his own blood. He had been shot. He was dying. He was losing consciousness.

The tide was going out on Chunk DeLuna. He saw himself sitting at the water's edge. He was dreaming of a day long ago.

*******

Life had come to an end for Chunk DeLuna. He lay in a pool of his own blood in his office at the CDL Cement plant in Olinda.

The custodian who came in at 7 a.m. discovered his body and called the police. The detective who arrived with three other officers made a determination he had been shot several times in his torso. Lieutenant Oscar Omera, the detective, was well familiar with Chunk DeLuna. Early on Omera had arrested DeLuna several times only to see him set free as charges were invariably dropped. Omera learned over time the influence, even as a young man, that DeLuna wielded.

After years, tired of fighting the corruption, Omera joined it— not in a big way. He just turned the other way on some crimes, was added to a weekly payroll of payoffs, and ultimately told DeLuna, "I will only look away for so long. If you commit a major crime in my city, you will go to jail." Drugs, gambling and prostitution were not major crimes to Omera; murder was.

Now here before him lay his benefactor and nemesis. Murdered. This was a serious crime to Omera. In the coming days, he would begin compiling a list of suspects, a number of whom he could pull up from memory. The list of suspects would include the Salvadoran drug dealer whose sister DeLuna had decapitated; the senator from Amazonia state whose daughter DeLuna killed in an acid bath; family members of former presidents of Olinda Cement who met violent ends; and leaders of rival gangs whose members were murdered—shot, hanged, drowned—by DeLuna in drug, prostitution and gambling wars. Members of DeLuna's own gang had motivation. Carlos appeared at the top of Detective Omera's list; for when Omera went to interview Carlos, the results of the horrific beating DeLuna had administered in a rage were apparent. "I fell down a flight of stairs," Carlos told Omera, who knew otherwise. He had heard about the beating from an informant in DeLuna's gang.

"Nice try, Carlos," Omera replied. Omera knew Carlos quite well. It was Carlos and sometimes Raphael who made the weekly payments to him. The Carlos he saw on the day of the interview was a different man from the confident, jovial person he knew.

It was Carlos who helped point Omera in the right direction to look for DeLuna's killer. Not so much by telling him where to look but by telling him, "You ask me who killed the boss? It wasn't any of us, and it wasn't his rivals. We were all too afraid of what would happen if we didn't succeed. For us, the boys and me, we loved him and we hated him. He saved us from nothingness. But he was tough when we screwed up or confronted him."

Right then, Carlos made a gesture, sort of indicating his appearance. Not pointing to himself, but his fingers moved inward, towards himself, in a small almost unintentional way. Omera picked up on it and knew the truth.

Omera continued their discussion, "Then if not a gang member or rival, someone closer? Three shots, close range, facing DeLuna. Someone he knew, trusted maybe?" Carlos said nothing further.

Next, Omera talked with Lupe. There was a faded bruise beside her left eye. A punch from DeLuna he thought. But after an hour of discussion with Lupe, Omera concluded it was not her. While she had expressed she was growing tired of his ways, she was grateful for all DeLuna had done for her; Omera saw a genuine sense of loss; she did not kill DeLuna.

Omera tracked leads relentlessly over several months. He heard heartbreaking stories from relatives whose family members DeLuna had slaughtered in one way or another, but no prime suspect came to the front of the investigation. Either believeable stories, "I wanted to kill him, but then I'd be just like him," from one parent of a slain prostitute or alibis left Omera with nothing five months after DeLuna was killed.

At six months, as Omera started boxing up his notes and files for cold case storage, he read through his earliest interview notes one more time. There was something in Carlos' interview, in the notes Omera had written that caught his attention: "C. seems to indicate not any of the gang or rivals. Maybe not saying, but maybe knows more?"

Omera remembered writing that. He didn't follow-up further with Carlos. At the time he believed Carlos was telling him where not to look. Dumb. If he knew where not to look, he probably also knew where to look.

Carlos agreed to come in to police headquarters, on the plaza atop the Olinda plateau and across the street from Sao Pedro church. Omera watched him from his office as he approached the building. His face had healed, and a swagger was back in his walk.

In the months since DeLuna had been killed, crime diminished significantly in and around Olinda. For the first time in years, there had been no murder recorded in the previous three months. Omera by this time had stopped taking weekly payoffs. Carlos, who took over the gang after DeLuna's demise, knew the rules and played much better with others.

"After your boss was killed," Omera began after they shook hands, a bit awkwardly between former payer and payee, "when you and I talked, you told me where not to look: at your gang or your enemies."

"That's right; I remember that."

"I figured at the time, with that lead, the answer would become apparent to me who killed DeLuna. But it has not."

"Sure, I thought you would have solved it quickly."

"But I didn't."

"You didn't. Correct."

"So now I need your help. You knew who didn't do it. So I should have asked the obvious question: who did do it?"

"At the time, I didn't care if you found out. I was pissed. Chunk was dead."

"And now?" Omera asked.

"Oscar, things have changed."

"Enlighten me," and to add to proper decorum, Omera added, "And Carlos, in here don't ever call me Oscar. It's Detective Lieutenant Omera."

"Yes."

"So enlighten me?"

"What I'll share with you, you can't act on. Things changed. People's lives changed—for the better."

"I'll decide that," Omera stated rather firmly.

"No, we're all in this together. I can share it. You won't be able to prove it nor will you want to. But, Lieutenant," Carlos said, emphasizing Lieutenant somewhat sarcastically, "I need your word nothing will happen to the person who killed Chunk."

"You know my rules. Almost anything goes but murder!" Omera said rising a bit in his chair, leaning in and emphasizing his own word, "murder!"

"You won't see this as murder," Carlos said calmly.

"Murder is murder. Taking another person's life is murder."

"You draw a funny line, detective. Addicting someone to drugs for the rest of their life is every bit the same."

"Don't you preach to me. These people are making choices. Murder is final. Even DeLuna didn't have a choice. His life was taken from him."

"He was my brother, my father. Chunk was everything to me. But he did a lot wrong in his life, more than any of us. More than all of us. More than any of us ever expected."

"What are you saying?" Omera asked, puzzled by what Carlos was trying to tell him.

"He stepped over the line, far over the line. So many times that we all knew this would happen someday. It wasn't that we wanted Chunk dead—he was key to our operation."

"His violence, you mean."

Carlos nodded. "His ability to impose his will by whatever means. And yes, frequently it was through violence."

"And?"

202

"And what we all knew would happen, happened. But the people involved are not bad people. They're good. This may be the only bad thing they've ever done."

"Carlos, it doesn't matter. The law is the law. Murder is murder. Worse than all other crimes put together. If you steal you can make restitution. If you gamble or lie with a prostitute, you can stop. If you're addicted to drugs, you can get help. But murder," and the detective turned it into a question for Carlos. "What can you do about murder?"

The two men looked at each other. Neither was going to change his mind. Carlos refused to tell the detective what happened and who killed DeLuna without the promise from Omera that he would do nothing.

Not yielding, Omera, kept the case open. He put additional surveillance on Carlos and on Lupe over the next two months.

Carlos continued with his businesses. Gambling and prostitution were a growth industry, and drugs had become more widespread with rival gangs moving into Recife and Olinda. Detective Omera attributed that to the absence of DeLuna. The murder rate was starting to increase as rival gangs battled for turf. Most surprisingly, the CDL Cement's business was flourishing thanks to an Olympic study and state of Pernambuco investigation into the partial collapse of Manaus Stadium and the role CDL Cement played in it. Both the study and the state investigation exonerated CDL Cement and stated the company could not have known about the underground river's eroding influence on the limestone formation that supported the great weight of the stadium. The investigation concluded that the surveyor who said the ground was sinking was seeking revenge for his dismissal. Nowhere in all the documents from the Manaus stadium project management records were there any survey readings even a millimeter different from the original readings taken in 2010.

Detective Omera had a bit more appreciation for DeLuna as Omera's plate was now getting full of unsolved homicides. With DeLuna around, there was a sameness, a sadistic sameness to the murders, and they only took place outside of Olinda. DeLuna played by Omera's rules—"anything you want, but no murders in my town." These new punks, Omera thought, kill on a whim. They send no message. There was always a purpose behind DeLuna's killings, and they always sent a message. He was not impulsive; he planned and executed. Omera, sighed, as he wished for the good old days.

As for Lupe Montserrat, the feedback Omera received was that she had a routine existence. She continued with her painting, and she moved to a high rise she owned on Boa Viagem beach facing the Atlantic.

Detective Omera thought about this information. Lupe was a beautiful woman, not yet thirty. The report stated that her painting instructor, an older gentleman named Estephan Kelly, stayed at Lupe's apartment one night a week. Yet he remained married, a long time successful marriage, inquiring officers were told.

"Lucky old dog," Omera said aloud, as he packaged the files in a cardboard box and wrote "DeLuna, cold case" on the outside.

# 33

It had been eight months since Chunk DeLuna was murdered. Lupe had transformed the oceanfront home where she and Chunk had lived into an art gallery for Estephan Kelly. Cars were overflowing into the winding drive that led to the circular front of the house. A parking area to the left was added and was full as patrons of the arts were flocking to see the works of the recently heralded "Lost Picasso of Brazil."

The *Recife News* had run an article in the arts section the previous week about the "exquisite treasure trove of work by Estephan Kelly, the Picasso of Brazil." It went on to describe Kelly's withdrawal from the world of art sales and how little by little over the course of the past six months, "Kelly has let us peek into the world he exiled himself into for the past twenty-five years. And what a wonderfully glorious world it is! Slowly, he has unveiled one stunning masterpiece at a time. Now, many of these masterworks are on display together. We and all of Brazil have come to realize what a magnificent collection of his own masterpieces he had been hoarding."

The article went on to say, "Kelly doesn't like the word "hoarding," he prefers "withholding," without explaining the nuance intended."

In the art crazed cities of Rio and Sao Paulo, a larger article ran in both cities' main newspapers, written by the famous Argentinian artist, Camile Cantanzaro. The gist of the article suggested that every man, woman and child in Brazil should rush to the seaside gallery showing these works. "Fourteen rooms are filled with over 150 paintings by the greatest artist South America has ever had. The building, which is guarded round the clock, has state-of-the-art alarm systems attesting to the value that lurks within." On the front page of both papers were pictures of three paintings on display. One was of a great mural of the Amazon jungle that had been moved from an entire wall of the artist's prior studio to the large salon in the gallery. It was estimated it had a value of $75 million and had been sitting unguarded in the studio for twenty years. Another picture was of a woman. "She is standing tall and straight; she has big hair with a part on the right. Her face is strong with high cheek bones and a straight nose. Her skin is Brazilian olive, and it has texture. She has a smile on her face, a full smile of bright white teeth between full lips."

"Kelly said the painting was of his wife, who died three weeks ago. He said he had painted it forty years ago when they were first married."

The third painting was drawing raves from the world of modern art. "A Brazilian Warhol," the article said, quoting a New York art critic who had just seen the painting. It was of two giant sets of lips kissing. "*The Kiss* is the most sensual piece of art ever created," raved the critic. "You can feel the emotion at the point of the impact of that kiss."

# 34

Not long after Estephan Kelly had been installed as the icon of art in Brazil and beyond, a funny thing happened. He became significantly wealthy from the sale of five of his paintings. He was represented by Sotheby's in New York and Sao Paulo. In back-to-back auctions by that house, his painting captured the top bids—one selling for $18 million to a Chinese businessman and one selling for $63 million, to, it was suspected, a Saudi oil prince.

The art world was shocked. Never had an unknown or lost artist commanded those prices so rapidly. It was universally acknowledged and understood that Estephan Kelly was an exceptional exception.

Lupe had two assets in her name—the houses—the ocean side mansion that she turned into the gallery for Estephan and the condo. Every other asset—cars, bank accounts, the cement company—had been in Chunk DeLuna's name and had or were in the process of being seized by the government. The government even found a secret DeLuna account in Rio.

Even as he became famous, he dutifully returned home to his wife every night, except for one night a week he would spend at Lupe's condo. When his wife died suddenly, Kelly stayed in the apartment they shared for another seven months. He bought the Oceanside gallery from Lupe for $3 million in cash. Three months after that, he moved in with Lupe to the condo on Boa Viagem beach.

Every morning Lupe and Estephan walk the beach at 6 a.m. Lupe swims in the ocean on Tuesday and Thursday afternoons. Estephan paints five days a week in his old studio as a professional staff sells his creations out of the oceanfront gallery. Lupe still takes lessons on Monday and Friday afternoons along with other students at Estephan's studio. Occasionally, the back bedroom is still used after other students leave. There is an old heat there that can't be replicated elsewhere. Estephan says it is the only reason he still keeps the old building. They still laugh loudly over their fortune, not the financial one, the one that found them, the one that enabled that first kiss. And on Wednesday afternoons Lupe goes to Boa Viagem beach and sits for a while in the sand. She blesses herself and says a prayer for Chunk—every Wednesday. She thanks God for two things: Chunk's care for her and deliverance from Chunk. She asks God to go easy on Chunk. She doesn't know the whole story of what made him like he was, but she knows God did not intend to create the man who became the beast of Brazil.

# EPILOGUE

At 5 a.m. on the day she decided to kill Chunk DeLuna, she took the gun from the top of the closet while her man slept. She drove to CDL's offices in Olinda and waited until she saw DeLuna enter. Carlos came along ten minutes later. While she did not plan on seeing him, she walked in with him saying she needed to talk with Chunk.

DeLuna heard the two of them talking, recognized their voices and came out of his office.

Suzanne Cardoza reached in her bag and pulled out the gun. She walked towards DeLuna, who saw the determination in her face. He began to advance toward her and from a distance of five feet she shot him in the chest. He raised his bandaged hand and she shot him a second time.

"You fucking maniac. You broke Lupe's arm because she loves Estephan," she stopped walking and watched DeLuna trying to make sense of what was happening. "That's right; she loves Estephan."

DeLuna's face was contorted in anger and pain. He was still standing and took another step towards Suzanne.

"You bastard. You will never hurt Lupe again," and she fired into his chest again as he reached for the gun. DeLuna fell to his knees and then toppled over backwards.

"Suzanne, are you crazy," Carlos said, coming at her.

Suzanne walked by him, put the gun in her purse and left.

Carlos followed her out the door, calling, "Why?"

Suzanne stopped by her car and turned. "You of all people know why. That beast did not deserve to live. And I would do anything, anything, to stop him from hurting my friend Lupe again."

# WHERE TO FIND TOM CONNOLLY ONLINE:

Twitter: http://www.twitter.com/tomcontcg

Facebook: http://www.facebook.com/tom.connolly775

Linkedin:
https://www.linkedin.com/profile/view?121210778%2FTomConno
lly

Smashwords: http://www.smashwords.com/interview/tomcon

# Other Books by Tom Connolly

"The Adored:

Seven wealthy boys, all only children, become "brothers" for life as they grow from pre-school through the Brunswick School in Greenwich into successful adults. However, one of them may have committed murder when he was a teenager.

CJ Strong, a young black man, is in prison for the murder he did not commit. Strong believes he knows who is guilty yet remains silent.

It is the women these men love that determine their fate as lives unwind and virtues waver. Silvana DeLuna, the washer woman of San Blas, Puerto Rico has lost her man yet finds love anew with one of the "brothers," Naval Officer Traynor Johnson. Santa Alba, the beauty queen of Coamo, has moved into the heart of Eddie Wheelwright, displacing Valerie McGuire. Val is a brilliant Wall Street equity analyst, who is struggling, searching for the part of her that is missing.

***Coming this fall, look for "The Rusty Earring"*** Stamford Police homicide detective Vito Boriello is called in to assist the Greenwich Police department when the heads of six young women are found in a town park. Each head has one earring missing. Boriello, aided by his wife, Rosa, a police dispatcher who likes solving crimes with her husband, is on the trail of a sadistic killer who has been at work for 9 years.

212

# ABOUT THE AUTHOR

Tom Connolly was born in Cambridge, Massachusetts. He studied business administration at Northeastern University and organization development at Manhattanville College where he received his Master of Science degree. He served in the US Air Force for four years and was stationed at Ramstein Air Base, Germany and New Delhi, India. After a career with IBM he started his own firm, Thundercloud Consulting Group, primarily focused on higher education transformation. He and his wife, Kathleen, reside in Connecticut.

I hope that you enjoyed this book. As an indie author, I very much depend on your feedback to see where my writing is going. I would be very grateful if you would take the time to pen a review on the site you purchased the book. This will not only help me but will also indicate to others your feelings, positive or negative, on the work. Writing is a challenging profession, especially for indie authors who do not have the back up of traditional publishers.

www.ingramcontent.com/pod-product-compliance
Lightning Source LLC
Chambersburg PA
CBHW051501170626
46811CB00002B/586